SPEAKING OUT

SPEAKING OUT

TEENAGERS TAKE ON RACE, SEX, AND IDENTITY

SUSAN KUKLIN

G. P. PUTNAM'S SONS   NEW YORK

G. P. Putnam's Sons, a division of The Putnam & Grosset Group,
200 Madison Avenue, New York, NY 10016.
Published simultaneously in Canada.
Printed in the United States of America.
Book design by Joy Taylor

Library of Congress Cataloging-in-Publication Data
Kuklin, Susan.   Speaking out : teenagers take on sex, race, and identity /
Susan Kuklin.   p.   cm.
1. Teenagers—New York (N.Y.)—Case studies.   2. Interpersonal relations
in adolescence—New York (N.Y.)   3. Self-perception in adolescence—
New York (N.Y.)   4. Self-esteem in adolescence—New York (N.Y.)   I. Title.
HQ796.K75   1993   305.2'35—dc20   92-44288   CIP

ISBN: 0-399-22343-6 (hardcover)
10 9 8 7 6 5 4 3 2 1

ISBN 0-399-22532-3 (paperback)
10 9 8 7 6 5 4 3 2 1

First Impression

*This book is dedicated to the women and men
who devote their lives to the teaching profession,
and especially to two who supported me,
Ida Kravitz and
Simpson Sasserath*

CONTENTS

SPEAKING OUT

Introduction

AT an after-school meeting at a high school in New York City, students came together to air their grievances and talk about their differences and commonalities. The African-American students were vocal and the Asian students were quiet. At one point Russell Hirsch, the teacher who chaired the session, asked, "Why is it that the Asians are put on the defensive? Why aren't the Asians saying anything?"

Everyone looked to Yung Lam, an outspoken senior who is the president of the Asian-American Club. Yung stood up to address the group. "I'm not saying anything because I'm Chinese and I do not think that you guys would care what I think." A number of black students shouted, "That's not true. That's not true." Yung sunk back into her chair, her face reddened, and she refused to say another word.

Later I asked Yung why she stopped talking. She told me, "This meeting was to express our personal feelings. So how come after I say my own personal feeling, they say my feeling was not true. It's *my own* feeling. I was furious."

Yung mistakenly interpreted the African-Americans' outburst, "that's not true," as a repudiation of her beliefs and as an accusation of a lie, when in fact it was a sympathetic expression of support. When I explained the meaning of their outburst, Yung was shocked.

———

THIS book narrates events and feelings of teenagers in a multicultural public high school. To write and photograph it, I spent a year at the Bayard Rustin High School for the Humanities, often referred to as Humanities High, interviewing students and teachers, observing classes and school club meetings, and attending after-school activities. I specifically wanted to explore issues related to prejudice, stereotyping, and identity. And I wanted to examine how teachers treat this subject in the classroom.

Patricia Black, the superintendent of Manhattan high schools, and I once taught at the same school. When I called her, she suggested Humanities because it is the most culturally diverse school in the city. Racially it is one-fourth white, one-fourth African-American, one-fourth Asian, and one-fourth Hispanic. Many nationalities and religions are represented. Socioeconomically, it is diverse as well: the students range from the children of diplomats to the children of the homeless. There is a small population of high-functioning "special-ed" kids. Some of these students have learning disabilities, some have emotional problems, and some have both. (Special-ed students get instruction in a setting with no more than twelve kids in the classroom. Besides the teacher, there is a paraprofessional to assist the students on a one-to-one basis.) Put all these elements together into one overcrowded building and what do you get? For the most part, a surprisingly harmonious community that could serve as a realistic model for others.

The principal, Joan Jarvis, says, "Visitors at this school get a sense of community and family when they talk with our staff and our students. There is a great deal of caring about what happens to other people. And it's a very nicely balanced group. There is not a preponderance of one ethnic group over another, or one religious group over another." Mrs. Jarvis is the heartbeat of the school. Much of the school's success revolves around her hands-on policy. She seems to know everyone's name. Both the students and the teachers are comfortable approaching her.

The faculty makes a concerted effort to stop any conflict before it escalates. On my first day, Mrs. Jarvis introduced me to Jeff Schwartz, a biology teacher who works with the leadership class, and Russell Hirsch, an English and music teacher who is the coordinator of a series of events known as Project Harmony. Hirsch says, "We're trying to improve ethnic awareness, make people more comfortable living with others who are different from themselves, help them become aware of their own heritage, and give them a better sense of pride and self-esteem."

Within minutes I was in the classroom, telling Schwartz's leadership class about my project and collecting much enthusiastic input. The school newspaper ran an article about the book and explained how a student could contact me in order to set up an interview. Participants were told that they had the right to review their material, and some chose to be anonymous. I also wrote a memo to the faculty and asked if I could observe their classes when material relevant to my subject was being addressed.

Even though Humanities High did not have conspicuous race, religion, or gender-bias problems, I was satisfied that it would be the correct choice for an exploration of how kids see themselves and each other. This book is an attempt to go around the ugly headlines and vicious bias attacks currently in the news in order to look at subtle experiences that people typically encounter. Indeed, culture-based incidents were apparent, but usually on manageable levels: ethnic joking, who sits where in the lunchroom, stereotypical expectations. As in the case with Yung Lam, conflicts often arose when language barriers interfered with attempts at reconciliation or self-definition. The people in the book were willing to reveal incidents that they experienced as well as their own prejudices. Some were caught between the cultural traditions of their country of origin and their desire to become "Americanized." Others resented the pressures from the increased influx of others into the American melting pot. There are times when they showed less compassion toward the other groups, especially when feeling backed against the wall.

Teenagers are at a stage where their hormones are raging, everything is felt intensely, and they all are trying to figure out who they are. They must not only deal with how the world perceives them, but how their own world is changing. Consequently, as part of their emerging identity, the teens must learn to live with others in a multicultural environment. The high school years may be a last chance for them to learn how to respond to their dissimilarities. Once students leave an environment where they must function with one another's differences, they might return to a milieu where everyone is like them. They might revert to a more rigid and less tolerant way of thinking.

Although the teachers in this book make an effort to find and emphasize commonalities among the students, they are fighting a continuous battle. Stereotypes that can lead to prejudice have already been established by cultural attitudes, family bias, media exploitation of dramatic bias-incidents, etc.

In order to break down misinterpretations, Mrs. Jarvis and her faculty make a conscious attempt to include everyone in school activities and to give positive recognition to ethnic differences. Ethnic lunches and an ethnic dinner at the end of the year are annual social events. In March, the school celebrates Bayard Rustin's birthday with a special event called Ethnic Heritage Day.

The principal is always on the lookout for innovative programs that will help her "children." Project Smart deals with student conflicts by means of a mediation process that includes students, faculty, and parents.

There is another program that is worth mentioning, though not featured in the book. Every Friday morning, Dean Barbara Williams's American history class was taught by Saralee Evans and Julian Johnson, members of a group of volunteers who teach a course on racism once a week in fifteen New York City high schools. Saralee is a civil liberties lawyer and Julian heads a nonprofit organization called The Bi-Centennial Committee On World Hunger. The program was established after a very tragic racial incident, the shooting of a young black teenager, Yousef Hawkins, by a group of white youths in Bensonhurst, a mostly white, working-class neighborhood in Brooklyn. With the help of other interested professionals, mostly lawyers, Norman Siegel, the director of the New York Civil Liberties Union, set up a program made up of fifteen biracial teams who spent time talking to high school students about prejudice, race relations, and stereotyping. Julian says, "We want to explore some of our feelings and attitudes about people who are different from us."

Everything was not harmonious at Humanities High. Not every event worked. The kids argued, teased each other, and could be mean-spirited. They usually formed cliques based either on race or academic accomplishments. During my term at the school, however, I found that the more the students talked about their differences, the more they found they had in common. In spite of failures and misconceptions, there were some encouraging signs that if people can get to know one another before they are set in their ways, it appears they will have fewer resentments and prejudices. The schools cannot do it alone. Families, educators, churches, and communities must work together.

The Photographs

WHILE the high school served as a backdrop, the particular ideas and feelings of the students and teachers were the primary focus. Therefore I chose to concentrate exclusively on the participants in the photographs. To do this, I used white seamless paper along with strobes and screens similar to those used in fashion photography.

The participants were invited to wear what they were most comfortable in or what they thought would represent who they were. Some spent a great deal of time deciding about their clothing and hair styles while others simply showed up as is.

Ronald Bing, the assistant principal and magician extraordinaire, somehow found a space for me to set up a studio. Students acted as my assistants. After a quick course in studio photography, Laura Fitch became my indispensable assistant and organized the photo sessions. Lenin Crespo helped set and strike the lights. Ben Perez and Miranda McGrath also pitched in when extra hands were needed. They were great.

Acknowledgments

IT takes courage to allow a reporter unlimited entry into the goings and comings of a school. Joan Jarvis not only gave me access but made me feel that I was part of the school's family. The only thing I can write about Joan without becoming teary-eyed is that if she could be cloned we would all live in a richer world.

Russ Hirsch was very helpful in the making of this book. He, too, gave me unlimited admission to his classes and to the after-school club, as well as giving up his office to conduct private interviews. Sharing his students was a joyous experience. Barbara Williams, Jeff Schwartz, Lou Howort, and Mark Thompson unselfishly gave me their time, their insights, their classrooms, and their friendship.

Much to my regret, not all the students and classes could be included in this book. There are many behind-the-scenes people whom I would also like to thank: Pat Black, Ronald Bing, Barbara Brown-Cooper, Betty Sanders, Lynne King, Saralee Evans, Julian Johnson, Brian Lederman, and Lamar Holmes. And thanks to Don Kao, of Project Reach, Adeyemi Bendele Marson, of the Martin Luther King, Jr., Institute for Nonviolence, and especially Walter Nagel, of the Bayard Rustin Fund.

Marshall Norstein, a wonderful photographer, was supportive and even lent personal equipment when extras were needed. Linda Levine generously shared her comprehensive expertise in conversations while I was writing the book and insightful observations and suggestions after reading the manuscript. Theodora Lurie, Helen Bates, Ellen Levine, and Serge Gavronsky are good friends who also contributed excellent recommendations. I am particularly appreciative to my exceptional editor, Refna Wilkin, who gave me thoughtful, thorough commentary. As always, my husband, Bailey Kuklin, was there to encourage—and challenge—my assumptions.

This book is about people's perceptions of themselves and others. Like the school it depicts, it does not have answers. Perhaps the testimonies reported here will serve as models for discussion. Prejudice manifests itself through apathy and fear. We need to talk to each other. We need to hear each other. We need to care. I am especially indebted to the remarkable students and faculty who allowed me into their lives, into their souls—bumps and warts included. This is not *my* book, it is *our* book.

—SK

Caught in the Crossfire

Akilah

I LIVE in a part of Brooklyn that is not very integrated. You don't see many white people. Me, I'm a West Indian Puerto Rican. My mother's from Barbados, my father's from Puerto Rico. I went to a nursery school with mostly Haitian kids. They called me a "little white girl" and treated me with less respect. They didn't understand that just because a person has light skin, she is not necessarily white.

My father always picked me up from school. He looks like a redneck with his white skin and light hair. The other kids saw him and teased me cruelly for being white. I would run home to my mother, crying, "I'm a white girl. I'm a white girl." And my mother, who has very dark skin, didn't understand where I got such stuff.

She would sit me down at the kitchen table and pour black coffee into one glass and then milk into another glass. "This is me and this is your father." Then she would put the milk and coffee together. "This is you," she would tell me. "You're not white."

"Okay, fine, I'm not white." I'd go back to school.

"You're white! You're white! And we don't like you." Home again, crying, "You don't understand, Mommy, I'm white!"

My mother went to the school. The other kids saw this black woman who said she was the white girl's mother. Why is she black? Then they freaked out. At that age they didn't understand. Now I find it funny.

I don't look at people based on their skin too much. I look at a person for the person. I don't respect people who judge you by skin color. I've come to this conclusion because of past experiences.

When I was younger, Puerto Rican girls didn't like me because my mother was black, therefore I was not a full-blooded Puerto Rican. Black people didn't like me because my father was Puerto Rican, therefore I was not a full-blooded black person. I was caught in a crossfire.

I tend to be more comfortable with blacks because of my mother. Besides, black people tend to be more accepting. Now I'm eighteen, and my group depends on age, not color. I've dated Chinese, blacks, whites, Puerto Ricans, you name it.

My mother does not like me wearing gold. She thinks the big gold earrings and stuff like that symbolizes the ghetto. She thinks that the stereotype of a black person who wears gold is a drug dealer. I had a boyfriend who wore gold, but wasn't a drug dealer. That changed her a little, but she thought he was a hoodlum. I like gold, but I stopped wearing it to please my mother.

Then I started going out with a white guy and she yelled, "Oh, my God, you're going from one extreme to the other."

I caught a lot of flak from my friends who don't believe in interracial relationships. Blacks and Puerto Ricans are fine because they are both minorities. Besides, Puerto Ricans have a lot of African in them.

I never brought my white boyfriend home. I didn't feel comfortable bringing him to my house because I didn't trust the guys in my neighborhood. They wouldn't have harmed me, but if he came from the train station by himself, they would have messed with him or said something to intimidate him.

I had a friend who felt that it was wrong for me to be dating a white guy. She said, "After all the things that white people have done to us, I don't understand how you can do this." She was dead set against my seeing this guy. She threatened me with our friendship. I was hurt. If she couldn't be a friend just because I went out with somebody not of our race, then, hey, she's no friend. That's how I saw it. My mother agreed.

Eventually I broke up with my white boyfriend, not because of the racial pressure but because he was cheating on me. Just like any other guy. And, he was cheating on me with a black girl.

Akilah

My girlfriend used to say, "White people are different. They look different. They smell different." But when push came to shove, he did the same thing that any other guy would do. Cheat.

After that, I began dating a Chinese guy. One night we were on the #6 train, going to the Village. He was sitting close to me, but we weren't holding hands or being lovey-dovey because we were kind of tired. Some guy came up to me and tried to talk to me. He said, "How ya doing, light skin?"

I said, "Hold on, I'm with my boyfriend." And then it dawned on me that he never would have thought that I would be with a Chinese guy, as fine as he was. My Chinese boyfriend went away to school and we just drifted apart.

You have to go for a guy who treats you with respect and is intelligent. That could be from any racial group. It would be more accepted in my society if I stayed within my group, but then again, I like to rebel.

I'm not a nonviolent person. I wish I could say that I was quiet, but I'm not. I'm very hot-tempered. I used to get into fights in junior high school. After school, I would get a whole bunch of girls together and think I was the crème de la crème. I was also going through a lot of changes. I was trying to find myself. Did you ever notice that when kids are trying to find themselves, they go for the most messed-up group? Anybody that's doing something wrong, that's who they go to. That's exactly what I did.

My group went around robbing and stealing. I never robbed anybody. I swear on a Bible. "They" robbed girls with big earrings.

This is what I learned from my "hangout" buddies: It is easy to mess around with a white person because they're always going to back off. They fear anyone who is not white. If you call a black person a nigger, and you're not black, he's going to swing on you. If you call a white person a honky, and you're not white, he's not going to do anything. He's going to walk away. That's because white people are scared.

Take the Wall Street suits, the easiest guys to mug. And the women are just as easy. I remember a woman getting on the train at Wall Street. No one was on the train but me and a bunch of girls. We were laughing really loud and just being stupid. Now I've seen *thirtysomething* and I know that white folks laugh just as loud and act just as stupid as we do. We may look a little different with our big gold earrings, puffed jackets, goose hair, and whatnot, but we all act the same. Anyway, this woman was about to get on the train. She looked at us, clutched her purse, and ran to the next car. We laughed and laughed. Of course, my friends would have mugged her. They would have hit her a few times and laughed about it. They would do it because it was easy, because she was white, because they were mad at the world, and because they just felt like doing it.

It isn't really about race. It's more like, "I feel like kicking somebody's ass," and whites are easy. And you know they got money because they are coming from Wall Street.

I changed my attitude when I saw my friend get shot. I was in the ninth grade at the time. (A lot of this stuff nobody knows. Make sure my mother doesn't buy this book.) And these girls weren't my close, close friends. My closest friends and I are very much alike—very sophisticated, very mature. Anyway, we were at a reggae party and some girl recognized one of my hangout buddies. They started arguing over a boy, and, to make a long story short, she pulled out on my friend and shot her. I heard shots and hit the floor. I wondered who got shot. When I was told it was my friend, I was scared. I was afraid that that could happen to me. I've walked away from three fights this year. In fact, I haven't gotten into a fight in a year and a half.

When I first came to this school, I was really loud. If you stood on the first floor, you could hear my mouth on the fifth floor. I was loud, rowdy, gaudy. I was a kid. Now, I'm real serious.

I get my ideas from my parents or from just looking around. I've done a lot of black studies on my own. I've read everything you can think of on Harriet Tubman, Malcolm X, and Martin Luther King. That's because I identify more with blacks than I do with Puerto Ricans.

Before I got into this school, I was very prejudiced against whites. What changed me was meeting white people. Before, I met a few white people, but we never really, truly interacted. The first white girl I met at this school was really cool. We started hanging out together because we both hated the same teacher. And he hated us—equally. We wrote notes to each other and talked. She didn't smell any different, either.

The one white boy that I knew did smell different, but his mother was a health nut, so his family may have used a different soap. Maybe all black people use the same soap.

Now, if I saw a bunch of girls mugging and beating a woman, I'd call the cops. I'm not so dumb to get involved. On one hand, I could relate to those girls. They were wrong. But they don't realize why they were wrong. First of all, you shouldn't rob anybody. If you don't have what they have, you just don't have what they have. You have to work for it. Second, you shouldn't be beating on somebody just because they are weaker than you. If you really want a challenge you should fight somebody your own size. And third off, when you are angry and take it out on somebody else, that's the easiest excuse.

CHAPTER 1

"What's in a Name?"

Humane Humanities Club

THE bell rings. Another day at Humanities High comes to an end. Students who do not participate in after-school activities pour out of the main entrance. On the second floor the school's clubs are about to begin.

"Save the Whales fliers! Get your whales fliers!" hollers Nicolette, a junior in the Humane Humanities Club. The diminutive student is almost hidden behind a mountain of pamphlets and loose papers that she clutches in her arms. "Don't forget the homeless rally!" she tells her friends as they pull various pages from her collection. Nicolette plops the remaining jumbled bunch of papers on the teacher's desk, heaves a sigh, and stands on tiptoe in order to write the new address of Greenpeace on the board.

As the members of the Humane Humanities Club trickle into Mr. Hirsch's music room, they take seats in the half circle of chairs in the front of the room. A few students choose to sit in the back, near the window. Mr. Hirsch, who teaches both music and English, joins Ben, a Cuban-Greek-American, and Maya-Shanti (name changed), who recently arrived from Nepal.

Ben leans across Hirsch's chair to talk to a few of the club members who are already in their seats. "I was walking in the Village with three friends who happen to be racially different. As we were walking down Sixth Avenue, a man behind us said, 'That's really great. A white guy, a black guy, an Oriental guy, and a Hispanic guy all walking together.' Then he reached into his pocket and

gave us each twenty dollars. We thanked the man, but we really didn't want to take the money. He insisted. He said, 'No, no, there should be more of that in the world.' "

"Wow!" says Wendy, a large, fair-skinned junior with long blond hair and blue eyes. "I wish I could be so lucky. You know what happened to me once? My sister and I were on the subway and someone shouted, 'Look at the Jewess across the way.' I looked down. I didn't feel ashamed, but I felt ostracized. I hid the Jewish star that I was wearing. Then I thought, 'No,' and took it out of my shirt. I felt better once I did that. It was so weird. So weird."

By now Nicolette has finished with her announcements and the entire group is eavesdropping on Ben and Wendy's discussion. "Was he black?" asks Jason, who sits in the back of the room.

"What does that have to do with it?" questions Maya-Shanti. Jason turns to the window without answering. Carrie, the president of the student association, suggests that they continue last week's discussion of racism.

Miranda, a senior, is the "official" photographer for the yearbook and newspaper. She prides herself on being the eyes of the school. She says, "Ever since we talked about racism, I've begun to notice it. One day at lunch there was an Asian student who wanted to make a phone call, but she was afraid to go to the phone because there were a group of Afros standing around it."

Earlier in the week, Miranda had been taking photographs for the yearbook. She was looking for candid shots in the hall. She took a picture of some guys who hadn't noticed her, which was the point of the snaps. "Then some other guys wanted their photos taken, too. They started yelling, 'Take my picture . . . take my picture. . . .' I turned around for one second to ask a friend a question. The guys thought that I was leaving without taking a photograph of their magnificences. They hollered, 'Come here, whitey.' "

Miranda, who can hardly be described as timid, went up to them. "I'm not taking a photo of you because you called me whitey. Good-bye." Then she stomped off dramatically.

"Were they just joking or were they serious?" asks Lori. Born in China, Lori fights the stereotype that Asians are reserved, studious, and only care about things "Chinese."

Humane Humanities Club

"I don't know," answers Miranda. "It was their tone when they called me whitey."

Wendy has had a lot of experience with the word whitey. She attended nursery school through seventh grade in an all-black school. "I almost forgot my own name. People would call me Snow White or Snow Flake. It hurt."

For Miranda, the implication of "whitey" was profound. "Not only do others think less of me, but it undermines my own self-esteem. When that kid called me whitey I was so insulted. He was saying that I was different because I'm white, that I'm less of a person because I'm white. Whitey means everything has been handed to you, all the money, all the opportunity. It's true that some whites have more opportunity than other people. But that's not who I am. I didn't enslave black people. My family came from Ireland, Russia, and Hungary. We had nothing to do with it. I was so insulted."

Wendy tries to figure out why the term whitey makes her feel so bad. "First of all I'm not white, I'm pink. I'm Russian. I'm Jewish. I'm a young woman. I'm not white."

Ben says, "Racism is tricky. Let's say you're in the subway and you see a gang of black guys terrorizing people. The chances are that the next time you see a group of black guys who are not terrorizing people, you're going to assume that they are."

Wendy takes center stage. "I have a problem and I really would like your input on this because I'm starting to be afraid of it. Two months ago I would look at someone and say, 'He's my friend.' Now I look at him and say, 'He's my *black* friend . . . my *Asian* friend.' It scares me because I don't like to think that way. Now when I see someone walking down the street, I never think, 'What a nice jacket.' I think, 'He's black.'"

Nicolette raises her arms to the sky and screams, "Ugh! I hate all these assumptions. I hate all these stereotypes. I hear them day in and day out: Blacks steal . . . Hispanics sell drugs . . . Asians are smart . . . Ugh! I just hate that stuff."

Kavita, who was born in India, has been quietly taking in the conversation. She describes a lesson in her social studies class that centered on bigotry. "The students were arguing with each other about who was what race. Take Zuzu. Today they were talking about whether he was white or not.''

"Now that's really weird," says Wendy.

"Zuzu's family is from Lebanon. He's a Shiite. He said that he was white and the teacher said that he was not. I found my teacher really offensive and said so. The class ended in a screaming match."

"White" seems to be getting a rough going over during this session. Kavita confides that her parents taught her to avoid white Americans. "I was especially told never to marry one because my mother told me that a white American man would tease me. I grew up being scared of white people. But I didn't grow up hating them. I could really be a racist, but I'm not. I just don't understand. I think we should do away with all terms regarding race. It leads to too many differences."

Jason sits in the back of the room. He is all in black, from his ripped jeans, pea coat, and mesh stockings to his black fingernail polish. He says, "Isn't that denying people their identity?"

"No, it's not." Maya-Shanti jumps in for her friend.

Jason does not let Maya-Shanti off the hook. He throws back his long blond hair and reveals a cascading green front lock which shines in the sunlight. "If an Hispanic person rips me off and the police ask me to describe him, what am I going to say—'I can't stereotype the burglar'?"

Everybody is giggling at the illustration. Not Maya-Shanti, she's dead serious. "That is too specific," she admonishes him. "If you come to school the first day and the person sitting next to you is Hispanic, why can't you just say, 'I met a new friend today'? After all, you wouldn't say, 'I made a new white friend.' Never have I heard that expression."

Mr. Hirsch does not want this discussion to end the same way Kavita's social studies class ended. He says, "Behind many stereotypes is a kernel of truth. The danger sets in when a stereotype becomes a prejudice and people, because of their prejudice, won't change their views when the facts are to the contrary."

The class discusses Hirsch's statement for quite some time. Ever the teacher, he continues to raise the level of the discussion by introducing semantics. "Over the years names keep changing. Maybe they get worn out. A lot of

Asians feel that 'Oriental' is an offensive term. And yet the word simply is Latin for 'Eastern.' "

"But to us," replies Lori, "it sounds like a carpet, not a person."

Mr. Hirsch remembers the time when "Negro," which comes from the Latin word for "black," was an appropriate term. Then the term became "black." For a while it was "Afro-American," but that didn't sit well with some people, and so it became "African-American."

Hirsch says that his sister-in-law is a black civil-rights lawyer. "This topic is very important for her. She doesn't like the term African-American. She thinks it makes black people a subgroup in America."

Wendy tells about her best friend, who is half black and half white. She refers to herself as a mulatto. Wendy's mom became upset when she heard that. She thought it was offensive. Mr. Hirsch explains that "mulatto" goes back to the Latin word for "mule," which is half donkey and half horse. It's a crossbreed.

Kavita has a friend who is half Iranian and half British. When she referred to herself as a mongrel, Kavita was shocked by the characterization.

Jason, meanwhile, has turned toward the window. He finds the "whitey" stuff depressing.

This year there are no black students in the club because the African-American Club meets on the same day. All the activist black kids are members of that club. Everyone agrees that it's a pity and their presence would add to the discussion.

Maya-Shanti has a great idea. "Let's pick a neutral day and have this discussion with everybody. Mr. Hirsch, would you stay late another day and run it?"

"Absolutely."

Miranda leans forward, her hand raised, fingers fluttering. "Mr. Hirsch, Mr. Hirsch, there is something else I noticed that we need to discuss. I noticed that black people call each other niggers and that seems to be okay. Sometimes it's used as a compliment. But when a white person calls them that, it's no compliment."

Hirsch replies, "I don't like blacks calling other blacks nigger. It is an ugly term, derogatory in its very nature. Miranda has the same feeling about the term whitey. It is starting to become semi-acceptable. And that bothers me. To allow that word to seep into our day-to-day speech is very dangerous. There was one time that I heard it used, though, and I thought it was very funny. There was a Chinese basketball team playing a Harlem team in Chinatown. In the stands I overheard one black guy say to another black guy, 'Those Chinese niggers are really good.' ''

CHAPTER **2**

Humane Humanities Speaks Out

WHEN we consider stereotypes or prejudice, we usually think in terms of race, religion, or nationality. But there are many other prejudices—and they can be just as hurtful. Some students in the Humane Humanities Club share their experiences and outlooks.

Wendy

I DON'T remember when I started being fat. In the fifth grade I remember telling my friend Kelly that I weighed a hundred pounds. I had gone from ninety to a hundred. It was a milestone.

In elementary school I was teased for lots of things. I was asthmatic. I'd cough a lot and then throw up in class. Between the asthma and my last name being "Gross," the kids had a field day. Every class has a kid that the others see and say, "Yyyy-yuuuuuuck." That was me.

I started my junior high career the same time that the Howard Beach incident hit the news. What happened was a bunch of white guys chased a black guy onto the highway and he got killed. Everyone at my school, including me, was really angry about it. The kids went around yelling, "Howard Beach, Howard Beach." I was the only white student in my school. A lot of African-

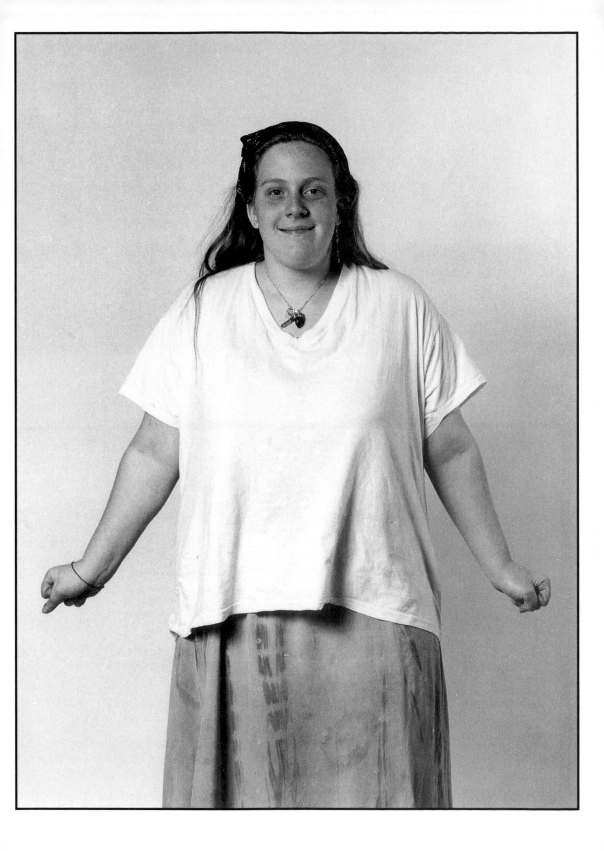

American people took their anger out on me. I'd be standing by the elevator and someone would walk by and yank my hair real hard. They would punch me or push me. This was the only way they could vent their anger and there was nothing I could do about it. I didn't want to fight back. Was that because I'm fat and have low self-esteem? I cried all the time. I was never angry at the African-Americans though. I was angry about Howard Beach, too. I guess I accepted getting beat up as a symbol.

I didn't tell my mom about it. There was a lot going on in her life and I didn't want to trouble her. Finally, I told her at the end of the year.

She said, "Oh, Wendy, I would have got you out of there in a minute."

My parents are divorced and my father is remarried. He has a little girl who is so cute. She is the only reason why I visit him. When I go to see my father in Connecticut, I feel very insecure. On the train ride up, I start to feel really bad about myself. By the time I arrive, I'm a bundle of insecurity. He harps on the way I look. He sees me for one weekend a year and feels that he can tell me what to do. We sit down to dinner and the first thing he says is, "You really should lose weight." Not that he does anything about his weight. Once I return home I use the trip to his house as an excuse to eat more.

Mom and I are really close. She wants me to lose weight and I want her to quit smoking. I know that if I badger her it won't make her stop, but she badgers me.

Other people assume that fat people just don't care and that's not true, because I've tried to diet a lot. Two years ago I stopped eating red meat and became a vegetarian. I was sure that I was going to lose weight because of it. But French fries are vegetarian and pizza is vegetarian. I didn't lose weight.

At a party everyone stands around eating junk food. After a while, they stop eating. I still feel like eating. I feel hungry a lot.

A lot of fat people eat when no one is around. I do that. I rationalize that if no one sees me eating, it won't count. I know that is a ridiculous excuse, but I do it anyway.

I associate losing weight with fixing all my problems. If I lose weight, I will be able to exercise more. If I exercise more, my asthma will go away. If my asthma goes away, I won't cough as much. If I don't cough as much, people won't tease me as much. Also, they won't tease me because I'm fat. Also, I will be able to find clothes. Yesterday, I made an announcement to my friends: "I'm going to Weight Watchers. I'm going to be thin, wear slutty clothes, and I'm going to tell everyone to fuck off."

Going into clothing stores is horrible. Recently, I desperately needed a new pair of jeans. I went to a store. The jeans there went up to size 14. Not big enough. The salesgirl said, "Oh, you can try on men's." I tried on a 36, 38, 40, 42, and none of them fit. First of all, it was exhausting. And secondly, it put me into a horrible mood. I ran out screaming, "Forget it. I don't want clothes! I'll go naked!"

Last year I got to know a college guy. Before we actually met, we had in-depth telephone conversations for hours. I told him things I never told anyone. He was really a nice guy.

He told me how he was into art and new-wave music. He said that people thought he was weird because he wears two different shoes. He was really cool.

He was always putting himself down, knocking his looks. When I finally met him, I thought, "This guy is not so bad." He was short, but not that skinny. He didn't seem too intellectual, he seemed more pseudo-intellectual.

The next morning he told me that my good friend Pat also talked to him on the phone. Then he said, "I seem to have a problem. I want to ask one of you out." I'm feeling, "Oiye." I don't like competition because I'm very insecure. I'm constantly asking people if they like me.

The second night this guy, Pat, David-my-very-best-friend-in-the-whole-wide-world, and I met at the Hard Rock Cafe for dinner. I paid $70 for all of us. Afterwards he told me about someone at college who he really loved. After practically making passes at me the day before, he tells me he's in love with another girl. What an asshole!

A few weeks after he went back to college, he called me up. We were talking about school stuff when he interrupted me. "Wendy, I called for a reason. I wanted to tell you why I wasn't attracted to you in the first place." I couldn't imagine what he had to say, but somehow I knew I was not going to like it.

"Wendy, I really feel that you are a fat shit."

"Huh?" I thought I wasn't hearing right.

He said, "Jesus Christ, you couldn't even fit into the table at the Hard Rock

Cafe." That was true, but the chair was up close against the wall. No one could have fit.

I couldn't believe he said that to me. "Don't you ever call me again!" I screamed and hung up.

Everybody said he was an asshole and I didn't believe them. Why didn't I see that? Why didn't I believe my friends? Am I that desperate to have a boy come on to me? Is it because I'm fat and he sees me as easy prey? I've heard people stereotype fat girls as being easy.

I'd really like a boy to like me for my looks. Let me rethink that. I'm so sick of being buddies with boys. I want a boyfriend. I want to get flowers on Valentine's Day. In summer camp I was "best buddies" with the guy that everyone was in love with. When we all went to Great Adventure, my best friend almost killed me because the cutest boy on the trip and I got lost together. Perhaps I'm best buddies with guys because they don't see a fat person as a romantic possibility. I'm safe.

Usually I think that I want to be thin to make it easier to get a boyfriend. But there are times when I say, "What do I need all this shit for?" I see my gorgeous friends crying and complaining about boys. Perhaps this boyfriend-girlfriend thing isn't worth it.

In a way, being thin wouldn't be good because I would be saying I couldn't live as a fat person. This is something I've thought about a lot. Maybe if I became thin I wouldn't appreciate things. I wouldn't appreciate my personality. I try to be a really good person even though I know that it doesn't always come out that way. There's a girl in this school who is fantastically, excruciatingly gorgeous. She's a model. But when you talk to her, she has absolutely nothing upstairs. If I become thin, will I be like that shallow person? When people win the lottery, do they change?

I have a friend who is bigger than me. I love to hang out with her, not only because I love her, and I do love her, but because she helps me feel good about myself. It's really pathetic.

Ben

WHEN I was two years old, my mom detected an oddness in my W's. It was very subtle, there was a slight pause before I spoke a W. I was forming the sound by saying W–wwww. She told her friends that I was going to be a stutterer. Her friends said, "No, everyone does that." They were wrong, she was right. I'm a stutterer.

Every morning I wake up and I'm still a stutterer. I face it as something I will do all my life, like shaving. That's the way it is. I've made peace with that. There are good days when I hardly stutter at all and then there are days when I'm tired and can't get a single thought out clearly.

When people meet a stutterer they immediately think that the person is dumb and insecure. I'm proof that that is not true. Stuttering is a disfluency in your speech. The air flow in your throat that is supposed to go out through your mouth becomes blocked. At some point your wind is cut off and you can't complete a sound. At least that is how it is for me.

In fourth grade if someone didn't like me, the first thing they called me was "stutterer." Kids would tease me: "Birds fly and butterflies flutter but all you can do is stu–stu–stut–ter." I would immediately go into a defense mode. I wouldn't talk, I would hit, hard.

I think that was a natural response for a nine-year-old who was not great about verbalizing his emotions. I couldn't talk about it the way I am talking about it now. In the sixth and seventh grades I wouldn't talk at all.

I'm a big guy now. Had I been smaller, physically, I would have been in a lot of trouble because I wasn't a great fighter. I got my ass kicked a lot. I was grateful when I grew. A bully doesn't want to mess with a big guy, so I now feel safe.

The most uncomfortable thing for a person who stutters is the listener. We die a little when a person who is listening to us go b–b–b–b–b–b–b–b–b–b is obviously wondering what to do. The best way for the listener to handle the situation is simply to wait until the b–b–b–'s are over. They usually don't wait. I've had people try to guess the word: Beast? Boat? Ball? It's terrible. I've had people just walk away. That's the worst.

My mom is Greek-American and my dad is Cuban. My father and mother married when I was two years old. If I hadn't been born, I don't think they would have gotten married. Not that they weren't happy to have me. My father often says, "You were unexpected but welcomed." I feel welcome.

In 1980 my father took part in the Mariel boat lift from Cuba. The boat lift that ferried people to the U.S. was big news at that time. For the boat lift, my father flew to Key West, built a boat all by himself, and sailed to Cuba. He brought back eight people, his entire family. On the way back, the boat sank and a huge chopper picked them out of the water and put them on an aircraft carrier. It was quite an exciting tale. I was six at the time. I was too young to understand how much danger my dad was in, but I was really proud of him. We had to pay a thousand dollars for every person he brought out. We sold everything to do it.

I was the only kid in my school who had a relative who was actively involved. Kids and teachers would stop me in the hall. "How's he doing? Have you heard anything?" It gave me a lot of self-esteem. In spite of my stuttering, I've never really lacked self-esteem. Even when I was failing I never lacked confidence.

In junior high school I was put into speech therapy. I learned the methods for controlling my speech: speaking slower and keeping my voice on. Keeping my voice on is a technique similar to those used by people who sing. When you sing, you never stop using your voice. I've learned to keep the air flowing and never let my voice stop. I apply the skill only when I need to. It really is a pain in the ass.

I came to Humanities last fall. Before that I went to Hunter High School, the most academically challenging public school in the city. People always thought I was really smart and I didn't want to risk proving them wrong, so I didn't try too much. My grades were terrible and my attitude was even worse. The only thing for me to do was to get out of the school.

The night before I started at Humanities, I cried myself to sleep. I had been a student at Hunter for eleven years. I didn't want to leave it, but I didn't want not to leave it, either. Changing schools meant leaving all my friends, everything that was familiar. I used to wear turtlenecks, corduroy pants, and sneakers all the time.

Ben

I woke up the next morning and I felt totally different. I went through a personality warp and completely changed myself. For my first day at my new school I put on a button-down shirt, a crew-neck sweater, and Dock-Sides. Oddly enough, I hate corduroy now. I don't think I had any dress sense. My grades went up. Now I have a 94 average.

I'm going to run for Student Association President this year. That's going to require a speech. I know that I can control my speech, but it's a pain in the ass to do it. I can't tell you how hard it is. Nobody wants to give a speech except politicians and they are weird anyway. I hate it but I'll do it anyway because I want to be president.

In this school I like to think that any girl who might be interested in me will overlook my stuttering. And they do.

I'm a success story, really. I can't give myself the credit. You can't get credit for something that you should have been doing all along.

Nicolette

I COME from a family of weird heights. There are tall people and short people and nobody in between. I'm 4′ 1.″ So is my mom. My dad's not the tallest person around, he's about average. My sister, however, is tall for a two-year-old. And my great-grandfather is six feet tall.

When I have a conversation with a group of people, the others are eye-to-eye and I'm always straining my neck upward. I was actually on the basketball team in junior high. I was the shortest member. I didn't get a chance to play much, but I still got an award for being on the team. I don't let my height get to me. Tall people have their limitations to some extent, too.

Because I'm short everyone calls me Munchkin. It bothered me at first. In the school play, *The Wiz*, I actually played a Munchkin. Now, when everyone calls me Munchkin, the name doesn't bother me. I even like it.

My friends always say to each other, "Hi, how are you?" Yet, when they see me, they just squeal, "Oh, cute and cuddly." It gets to the point where I yell, "Get away from me. Can't you just say hello? Must you pinch me on the

cheeks every time you see me?" I wouldn't mind it if they pinched everyone as a friendly gesture, but they don't. They just do it to me. They would never do that to a tall person. I want people to know there is more to me than cute and cuddly.

My father is a dental technician and my mother is a secretary. Our house is divided into various cultures. Each corner has a different culture. My parents' bedroom is Asian. They have bamboo furniture, antiques, and a little Buddha temple. The living room is full of European antiques and our bookshelves are filled with art books of different cultures and religions. My room, though, is a traditional teenage room with plain white walls and stuffed animals all over the place.

When we moved into our apartment we had it blessed by a rabbi even though we're not Jewish. We have a mezuzah on the door. (A mezuzah is a small case that holds a piece of parchment with religious passages on one side and the Hebrew word for God on the other.) When I was little I wore a sari (a lightweight wrapped garment worn by women of India and Pakistan). My parents try to integrate everything we eat and everything we do.

For our own culture, Hispanic, we go through these weird spiritual things, like blessing our house with holy water every year. This is an observance that my grandparents passed on to us. And once a year we go to church and pray for the souls of the dead.

There are certain superstitions that my family has. For example, when a woman is pregnant, she is asked to sit on one of two cushions. Under one cushion is a fork and the other a spoon. If she sits on the cushion with a spoon, that means she will have a girl. If she sits on the fork she will have a boy. I think these superstitions are funny. My mother sat on the fork cushion and she was sure she was going to have a boy, even after the medical reports had already told her that she would have a girl.

Kavita

AFTER school I go to museums. I respond to surreal paintings. I look for myself in the paintings, in the colors, in the objects. I look for God in the paintings. I look for God in me.

Most people know nothing about Indians. They assume that all Indians have heavy, singsong accents and work in Seven-Eleven stores or in newsstands. I speak English without an accent. My parents met when they came to America as members of the diplomatic service.

I've only been going to Humanities since October. I used to be a student at Hunter High School. For the last few years I've had lots of problems that center around my family. My family thought that the stress at home along with the stress of an academically tough school was too much for me. So I came here. Coming here is even worse than enduring the academic pressure at Hunter.

Some of the kids around here call me a nerd. There was a volleyball game this year between Hunter and Humanities. I was sitting with my friends from Hunter and wearing a Hunter T-shirt. Members of the Humanities team saw me and called me a traitor. In one afternoon, I went from being called nerd to traitor.

I know that it is prejudiced of me to say this, but I am used to the elitism in my other school. I'm not used to being around people who don't study and don't care. When we take a test, the other students scramble to sit next to me. One person will look at my paper, copy the answer, and pass it on to the next student. Three or four people get my answers. I can't say anything to my teacher because that would make the situation worse. It doesn't matter. They never copy the answers right, they get them all confused. At one time I got very good grades. Hundreds. Now I don't.

People think that Indians are all one specific race, but in fact we are many colors. My American history teacher told me what race I belong to. She said I was Asian because I was from India. There is no race called Asian. I argued with her, not because I didn't want to be associated with certain people, but because it wasn't true. With the exception of Wendy, the whole class hated me for taking up the time. The teacher said that I was being a racist for saying I

wasn't part of such-and-such a race. What could I do? I'm not going to let the whole class believe something that is not true. Then the teacher said that a person of color doesn't have a chance in politics here. That got me so depressed that I gave up on school.

People don't know much about Indian culture. They put all of us into one religious group: Hindu. I'm a Sikh. In this school no one understands what it means to be a Sikh. In my religion, the men wear turbans and they have beards. Both women and men are forbidden to cut their hair. We must carry a symbolic knife, a dagger, on our person at all times. I guess when the religion was established there was a war so they needed the dagger for protection. I used to wear a small gold dagger on a gold chain but I took it off because people used to look at me like I was weird. They'd ask too many questions.

In my parents' generation, most Indian marriages were arranged, but theirs was a love marriage. Before that, my father had had an arranged marriage. He and his first wife had two children. After his divorce, when my parents married, his children moved in with them. Then my cousins, uncles, and aunts moved in as well. They all lived together in a small apartment. There was only one decent bedroom. I have no idea how they managed.

My mother was fifty years old when she found out that she was pregnant with me. She thought she was going through menopause. Then she didn't want to be around the extended family because our household was kind of violent. My mother left and stayed with her Hindu Guru in India so that I could be born in an ashram. Two months after I was born, we returned to New York.

The culture gap between my parents and me gets in the way. It is such a strange, complex thing. They grew up under British rule. Everything that was British was good and clean, but they still hated the British. They are against Americans, but when they want to prove something is right, they say, "This is the way the Americans do it." They are so illogical.

My half sister is married and has been living in Iowa for sixteen years. Hers was an arranged marriage, too. I see that she is happy, but that kind of life is not for me at all. The way they pick a husband or a wife in India is really shallow. Everything depends on each person's financial background.

When I could no longer stand living with my parents, I moved to Iowa to live with my sister. She was even more strict than my parents. She wouldn't let

Kavita

me go out of the house. I was fifteen years old and had no privacy. It was awful.

People in most places are afraid of people who are different. In my sister's small town in Iowa, I was a lot different. First of all, the people were prejudiced about my being from New York. They asked me about the drug situation there. I thought that was so hypocritical because the only thing the kids did in that town was drink and party. I told them that I didn't party much because I spent all my time at home or at museums. They thought I was crazy. They didn't understand how I feel when I'm looking at a painting or a sculpture.

Secondly, some of the people there were so stupid they didn't even know where India was. There was one person who asked me where I was from. When I said I was Indian, he thought that I meant Native American. He started going on and on about how sorry he was that the white man had come and taken away our land. I tried to explain that I was not a Native American, but still he didn't understand. So I just smiled. I was so embarrassed for him.

My worst experience, though, was when a guy in a gas station called me a nigger. Here's how it happened. There was a clothing store that would only allow five kids in it at a time. I was with a group of black kids who were waiting just outside the door when a woman tried to go inside. I didn't get out of her way at first because I didn't realize that she was there. This gas station worker, who was walking by, started yelling at us, "You niggers, you black kids, you don't know your place."

I followed him into his garage screaming, "Who the hell do you think you are—you, a gas station worker—to say you are superior to me, a public school student?" I told my sister not to go to that gas station, but she paid no attention to me. I felt betrayed.

CHAPTER 3

Views from Far Away: Hong Kong, Kathmandu, & Queens

SOME students, such as Wendy, Ben, Nicolette, and Kavita, struggle with prejudices against people's individual, personal characteristics. Other students, Lori, Maya-Shanti, and Jason, must contend with preconceptions about groups and cultures.

Lori

THIRD period. Public-speaking class. Lori is about to give a speech about prejudice. She has been working on her two-part speech for weeks. Part I is filled with historical events, such as the intolerable bigotry faced by the Chinese laborers at the turn of the century when they came to America. Part II is about the personal experiences Lori's Chinese friends and family encountered as immigrants in the twentieth century. About halfway through her speech, Lori stumbles on a few words. Then she loses her place. Her face reddens. Long pauses. Embarrassed silence. The pages of her speech become all jumbled up. Tears pour from Lori's eyes. She stops trying, sits down, puts her head on the desk, and cries. The teacher handles the difficult situation just right and no one snickers. It is hard to give a speech in front of a group of peers, and the other students commiserate with Lori's plight.

WHEN I was reading my speech, everything was going okay until I got so emotional. I came to a part where a black kid told a friend of mine to go back to where she came from. My friend couldn't do anything about his comments because she was afraid of him. Even though the incident didn't happen to me personally, I really felt it. I wouldn't fight back, either, because I would be afraid. That's why I started to cry. It wasn't because I couldn't do the speech. I practiced that speech a lot. It's painful to me that someone would get hurt just because she's Chinese.

I'm from China. We used to be really poor. In China, poor people were treated very bad. I came here twelve years ago when I was seven years old, so I don't remember much. My parents work in a factory. I have two siblings.

I'm one of those people who you need to get to know. If I don't know you, then I'm not too friendly. Once I know you, I make jokes and I go crazy. When I first came here I didn't know much about this school. I didn't know what to expect. Very quickly I met many people from other countries like Nepal, Hungary, Yugoslavia. I love to listen to my Hungarian friend talk about what life was like in Hungary. My black friend, Rasheeda, told me all about the African cultures. I found it much more fascinating than my own culture.

Most of my Chinese friends stick with their own crowd. I find it offensive when I'm talking to a friend who only speaks English and a Chinese person comes up to us and speaks to me in Chinese. I say, "Why don't you speak to me later." My Chinese friends get pissed when I say that. They do not consider it rude, as I do.

I work as an assistant in an after-school project for little kids. One day the kids were making fun of Chinese people. They were just making faces. They were pulling on their eyes. The eyes business bothers me. I got mad and screamed at them, "That's not funny!" When someone makes a remark about slant eyes, it is very offensive. It makes me feel that I don't belong here. It makes me feel that I'm an "other."

There was another time when two black kids were fighting. One pushed the other one down. When he got up, he said to me, "Get that nigger out of my

Lori

face." I screamed at him, "No, don't you even dare say that!" Everyone looked at *me* like I was crazy or something. I got really mad. A black teacher came up to me and asked what that kid said. When I told her, she said, "Oh," and walked away. Then I went to the leader, a white teacher, who sent the kid away. Why must everything come down to race?

I like this school. Everyone is really friendly. But lately things started happening. Stupid little things that get in the way, like the blacks pushing Asians around. The Humane Humanities Club used to deal with environmental issues. This year they started to deal with prejudice and things like that. Before that, I didn't know there was such a thing as prejudice in this school. Now, I find that I'm looking at what race a person is. Is she an African-American? Is he Hispanic? White? Asian?

I know that prejudice is one of those things that we have to face. But I wish that the club didn't talk about it so that I wouldn't have to know about it.

Maya-Shanti

I COME from the other side of the world, Nepal. I'm torn between two cultures. I'm isolated. I feel really bad about it.

In Nepal we live by a caste system, an ancient social system based on a person's birth. Roughly speaking, castes range in the following order: first, the priests (Brahmin), then the warriors and princes (Chatriya), then the merchants, farmers, and business people (Vaisha), and finally, the workers (Shudra), who do the cleaning and things like that. These four basic divisions have divided into many subcastes. Caste is no longer part of the law, but people continue its tradition.

My father is a Chatriya and my mother is a Newar, a subcaste of the Vaishas. People look up to my father's caste. In fact, even the King of Nepal is a Chatriya. The Newars, who are merchants, are considered crude. The Chatriyas make fun of the way they talk and deride them as "shrewd, like Jews." Among the Chatriyas, they are considered bad company.

The Newars, however, are very wealthy. They are the first inhabitants of the

Kathmandu valley. (The Kathmandu valley is the richest part of Nepal.) Because they consider themselves special to the valley, they do not want any other caste to marry into theirs, even the higher castes like my dad's. You could say that my mother's caste is more like a tribe.

When we moved to the U.S., I learned that you have a system similar to our caste system, only yours is based on physical appearances. Here, the white people are the rulers, the Chinese people are the brains, and the black people do the labor.

Since this is a developed country, it sounds so primitive to judge someone based on the color of one's skin. In Nepal, I blame their primitive notions on a lack of education. Even the educated people don't question much. They do something because they've been doing it for generations and generations. In the U.S., the schools are free and everyone can get an education. I hear the students at this school ask questions all the time. Yet there is still prejudice. In some ways your country is very primitive.

I love this school. I've gone to many schools in three different countries and have had some difficult times. When I was three, my family moved to London. We lived there for five years. At my new school I heard people laughing when I couldn't pronounce certain words.

In London I developed a posh kind of accent. When my family returned to Nepal, my Nepali had changed because I had not spoken it much. Everyone laughed at me when I spoke Nepali. If I stopped speaking Nepali and started speaking English, the other children assumed that I was trying to show off. We lived in Nepal for eight years.

In my parents' day, theirs was one of the very few non-arranged love marriages. When they married, there was no one from my father's side (except one cousin, who is more like a friend) who would attend the wedding.

My grandmother never liked the idea of my father marrying a Newar. She only started to like my mother when we returned to London and my mother sent her goods from England. Even then, my grandmother preferred my aunts who were pure Chatriya. They had arranged marriages.

Even to this day, my grandmother favors my cousins. In some ways I am my grandmother's favorite grandchild because I am the youngest. But when it comes to important matters, she never includes me. She asks my cousins their opinion, but she never asks mine. She buys my cousins many outfits for our festivals and holidays, but I have received only one outfit for a special festival.

I don't know much about my mother's family. They didn't want anything to do with us. I'm not sure why.

Five years ago my mother died. I was eleven. After she died, the littlest things became so big. When I needed to wear a bra, I didn't have a woman to talk to. My mother wasn't there and my sister had married and moved far away. I couldn't talk about that to my father. My mother had told me all about the mean things my aunts used to do to her because she was of a lower caste, so I didn't want to go to them. And you never talk about personal issues to teachers in Nepal like you do here.

I took over the job of entertaining for my father. Even though I was too young to handle parties, I wanted to make him happy, so I tried. You know how hard it is just to have a few people in your house. Everything is even harder in Nepal. I was a kid, but I took charge of the house all by myself. At least there were people hired to do the housework.

When my father was appointed to the United Nations and we made preparations to move to New York, I knew that I had to switch gears all over again. In New York there would not be a staff available to do our housework. I would have to do it. Since school starts early in New York there would be no one to cook my father's breakfast. We talked it over and decided that the best thing for all of us would be for my father to remarry. My new stepmother is a Chatriya. My grandmother arranged the marriage.

I was so glad when my father got married. Before, I felt like I was a housewife and I really didn't want to be that.

My older brother is totally into the American system. My dad doesn't worry about my brother. I can't have a boyfriend, but my dad doesn't say anything when girls call up my brother. Girls call him at twelve o'clock at night and my father thinks it is funny. But if I got a call from one boy, he'd inquire about every detail. That's why I've never had a boy call me at home. I've never taken a friend home.

Even though we are in America, my dad still expects certain Nepali things of us. For example, he wants us all to have dinner together. We have dinner at ten o'clock because we must wait for him to finish work. And sometimes he phones us at ten o'clock to say that he will be late. We then must wait even later so that we can have dinner together.

My dad's such a nice person. I admire him so much. Whenever he says something to me, I never argue. And he's so nice I don't want to push. The only thing I have ever pushed him on is the school play. I want to be in it so badly. Every time I ask him if I can be in the play, he changes the subject. He tells me that it is my bedtime or that he is busy watching a movie. This has been going on for a month. Yesterday I finally talked to him about my being in the play. He said that he didn't want me to stay after school late. I told him that the rehearsals will be on weekends. He said, "Weekends are time you spend with your family. If you are in the play you won't have time to spend with your family. You make the decision." I really do want to be in that play, but I get this guilty feeling. What can I do? I know that the real reason why he does not want me to be in the play is because he doesn't want me to act on the same stage with boys.

When I lived in Nepal I knew the whole school and the whole school knew me. I was very popular and I even became the vice-captain. Here I'm not doing anything, not much at least. The reason why I am not doing anything much has more to do with my Nepali traditions than with my ability to make friends.

First of all I have to be home by six o'clock. It is not because my father doesn't trust me, he just worries. If I don't stay out late, I don't have the time to make friends. So I don't have a lot of friends. A second difference between me and American teenagers is that my dad doesn't want me to have a boyfriend. I don't object to that because he gives me good reasons not to have one. For example, he says it will have a bad effect on my studies. When I tell my friends that I've never had a boyfriend, they look at me with this big stare.

Third, I get good grades because I don't have anything else to do. If you answer correctly in class all the time, the other students think you are a nerd. Especially me, because I wear glasses. Double nerd. I would never show anyone my report card around here.

A lot of people believe the cliché that the Chinese students are studious and don't talk too much. The Chinese students feel the same way about me. At the Asian-American Club, some of the Chinese club members don't even bother to talk to me.

Jason

'M a member of the Humane Humanities Club because it needs me. It needs a different point of view. I come to the club with a feeling of dread and despair because we talk about so many things that are wrong and shouldn't happen.

So many things are unfair. All the emphasis is on the African-American person who is oppressed in America. What about the poor oppressed whites? Why can't I go into the lunchroom and shout, "I'm European. My forefathers conquered this land and I am proud of it." I can't do that because someone will call me a Nazi or Hitler's offspring. I can say I am Russian or I am English, but I can't scream out that I'm white.

I grew up in Whitestone, Queens. I got kicked out of my mother's house when I was fifteen. I migrated to my father's house in Manhattan and I've been sleeping on the couch ever since.

In the seventh grade I wore sweat pants with Ocean Pacific T-shirts, and listened to the top forty. My hair was short and spiked up. I was into mousse and gel. Getting a gold chain was my big dream.

Then came the eighth grade. By now the top forty were replaced by some heavy-metal bands. When I started bleaching my jeans in the bathroom, my mother said that I was falling into the grip of Satan. She said, "This is what happens when you don't go to church." I didn't go to church for a reason. I couldn't stand the hypocrisy.

I was never into Satan, never once in my life. I just junked the whole Catholic thing. Not that I don't believe in God. I do. I believe in an entity who has formed this Earth. I don't believe in a specific religion.

Anyway, if I walked the wrong way, my mother assumed that I was on drugs. If I woke up late, she assumed I was on drugs. I wasn't. I hadn't even started drinking then.

My drinking began a little after I started ripping my jeans, eighth-grade summer. Drinking was the thing to do with all your friends on Sunday or Saturday. The first time I did it, my friends watched in awe as I mixed equal parts vodka and orange juice. It was a dramatic moment. My friends wouldn't

Jason

drink with me. I drank the whole bottle of vodka. I thought it was supposed to taste that bad.

I got home three hours late. That is something you never do in my house. An hour later the house was spinning and I was afraid I was going to land on a witch somewhere. I got up and crawled to the toilet from my bedroom.

My mother, angry that I was late, called, "Jason, you're never going out again. You're grounded for a year." As I'm puking over the toilet, I replied, "Fine! Ground me for a century." At that moment I swore I wanted to stay in that bathroom forever. The next morning everything tasted like vodka.

Eventually, I started to semi-enjoy drinking. Also, I wanted to escape the basic oppression at home.

Everything in the house belonged to my mother, even my room and my stuff. If I said, "Mom, I'm going out after school," I had to answer twenty questions. Here I was living in Whitestone, Queens, a small neighborhood. What could I possibly do? When I went out the door, she'd yell, "Where are you going?"

"I'm going to the Alaskan pipeline."

My home was like an airport. You needed clearance to take off, you needed clearance to land.

The older I got, the less I saw of my father. He's a private investigator. They separated a million years ago. They have been divorced unofficially for ten years. He's been living with someone else and has a son. At one point my mom lived with someone else, too, but he died. I have a half brother from my mother's once-to-be husband.

My mother's entire family is working class. Originally they came from England. They believe in all that stuff about prestige, honor, and bloodline. I'm especially proud of my mother's heritage. I love it to death. I'm a big history-and-philosophy buff. My father's family came from Russia and there's not much that I know about them. They were Russian Jews.

I grew up with my parents making religious slurs about each other. And they *always* made them about me. Back and forth. Back and forth. My dad would say, "Catholic, up your ass." My mother would say to me, "You're just like your father. A spoiled Jewish bastard brat." The word bastard really got to me. It seemed really cutting.

The two families never liked each other. They took the stereotyping literally. My mom would say to my aunt, "See what I mean, they don't even show up for Jason's birthday party. That's because they're Jewish. Just like a Jew."

My mom always said, "Just-like-a-Jew. Just-like-a-Jew. Just-like-a-Jew." When people asked me about my roots, I used to skip over the Jewish part.

In my neighborhood if a black guy walks down the street, everyone's going to look at him. I look too, sure. If a white guy is in an all-black neighborhood, they're going to look at him. I know this for a fact. I once walked down the street in Harlem. Not only did they look at me, but they started screaming things and making fun of me. On second thought, I guess any neighborhood would make fun of me for what I look like.

When I was kicked out of my house, I was a miniature racist in my heart. On my block there was a public pool. The blacks used to come down my street to go to the pool. They didn't come from our neighborhood and this was a neighborhood pool.

They came in busloads. It bothered us. Are we rich millionaires who can share our world? It's a misconception that because I'm white I must have a Monte Carlo SS. My mom stopped going to the pool. After one summer no whites would go to the pool. It seemed like the blacks kicked us out.

I don't put green dye in my hair because I want to be cool and bad. No! My life is a festival. It's a big party that should be expressed. Now, I'm not making fun of people who conform. Some people choose to express themselves in different ways, like drawing.

No one at Humanities teases me. They just look at me and don't understand why. I get questions like, "Are you into Satan? Do your parents beat you?" They think that I am one of those people on *Twenty-one Jump Street,* like those punk kids who the cops arrest. I am probably the least violent student in this entire school. I have green hair, for God's sake. Do you think I could run away from a crime scene and no one's going to identify me? As a white youth, I feel like there is this cloud of guilt over me all the time.

I love the fact that I'm exposed to different cultures. But I don't like the fact that when I walk into a friggin' deli and ask for a pack of Marlboro, the man behind the counter has no idea what I'm talking about. I don't like the fact that when I call up for pizza and an Arab answers the phone, he gets mad at me because I don't understand what he's saying. I don't like the fact that I can be walking down the hall and two people in front of me are speaking in their home language and I don't understand what they are saying. It frustrates me.

I feel pressured. I feel squeezed. I feel threatened. I feel squeezed out by the Asian population because they are better workers than I am. When I come to school, my number-one concern is, "Are my boots laced straight?" The Asians make an arrow right for those books. Soon you won't see many whites on Wall Street like you do now. It will be all Asian.

I won't attend the Black History events, and, as a matter of fact, I resent them. It's all the emphasis on African-Americans that gets to me. I don't understand why the NAACP college fund is for blacks only. If I don't like a person—and God forbid that person is another color—that means I'm a racist. That pisses me off.

I have plenty of black friends. I have plenty of every kind of friend. I don't feel anger about anyone's race. I have a hard time explaining what I'm feeling. Some things get my motor going.

Now there is a group to help explain what I'm feeling. It is called the NAAWP, the National Association for the Advancement of White People. I'm a member. Their beliefs are not totally mine, because they have right-to-life views, and I don't. But I enjoy their literature. I'm also a member of the John Birch Society. Most of their ideals center around reverse discrimination. Take busing. I'm against it. It doesn't work to mesh two different racial groups together when there is no preparation for it.

I thought that when I moved to New York City, I could do anything. In all the movies I saw, people walked around in hot-dog costumes and no one paid any attention to them. I thought high school would be great. But now I know that this school is not so much a melting pot of expression as a melting pot of conformity. Now that I'm here I find myself just as lonely as I would be anywhere else.

CHAPTER 4

The President

Carrie

L ET me tell you about the chorus versus the drama club. It just so happens that the chorus is black and the drama club is white. There was even a letter to the editor of the school paper about that. This may be a stereotype, but in this school we simply do not have good white singers. Mr. Steward, the director of the chorus, doesn't want his kids to leave him and join the drama department. And I don't want the chorus to join the drama club, either. The blacks in this school really do sing better. If they come into the club, there is the possibility that the whites will be pushed out. There's an underlying tension between us. Meanwhile, Mrs. Jarvis, the principal, insists that we mix.

I'm in the school play. I have a lead part and I'm very happy about that. I hope no one takes offense, but there's a girl who's playing the other lead who was drawn out of the chorus. She's the best singer in the school. Now I'm scared and upset. We've always done musicals and we've always been mediocre singers. And it's been okay. We managed. I guess this is a real prejudice, but I don't want those people to come in and spoil the fun.

When a person sees something that is different, it becomes threatening. I'm beginning to see how that works even in the most subtle ways.

I'm not like most of the people in this school. I get better grades and am less apt to cut. Most of the kids are satisfied with average grades. The other kids are loud, have tons of friends, get together all the time, and are never home.

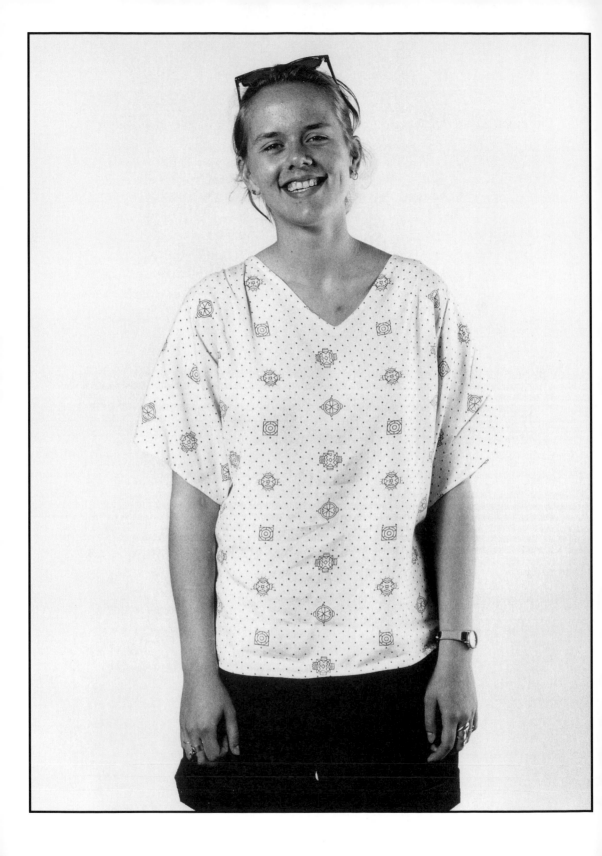

I'm quiet. I like being with my parents. Those would be my distinguishing characteristics.

I'm interested in politics and world events. I read *The New York Times*. I talk about heavy issues to my American history teacher, who is wonderful. And I spend time with adults. I do adult things. I worked on the Dukakis campaign. I go to the theater. I go to lectures. The kids here do not do that. Even my best friends don't care about such things.

Besides boys, we talk about other people, movies, makeup, and clothes. I don't mind because I don't want to always be talking about heavy, intense subjects like the Middle East or the Contras. It's nice to flake out and talk about boys.

The wonderful thing about this school is that no one has ever put me down for being the way I am. I never experienced any malice. I'm not sure why. It's more like, "Oh, of course Carrie did her homework."

People see me in the halls and say, "Hello, Ms. Abels." Everyone calls me "Ms. Abels." I ask them why and they say it's because I'm so mature.

I believe that the root of everyone's problems is that we never want to put blame on ourselves. We don't want to look at who we are because we are afraid of what we might find. I know what I want and I know how I want to live. I look at myself all the time. When I look, really look, I see that I'm not consistent, especially when it comes to race, religion, and politics. It's a dilemma.

My parents are very liberal. My dad's a theater director and my mom's a spiritual counselor. My parents taught me to love and respect everybody. Race and sexual orientation don't matter to my parents at all.

We're very Catholic. We go to church every week, but we don't agree with everything the Church says. It is too conservative for us. We want the Church to acknowledge woman priests and we want priests to be allowed to marry. We stick with the Church because we want to make it better. We want to work from within it. When we express our views in our church we usually get ostracized.

I'm very proud of my parents. My mom works for Pax Christi, the Catholic peace movement. She has been spit on by people who disagree with it. Even though we have the support of most of the congregation, we can't get church

Carrie

office space. The flak we get makes us stronger because we're such a religious family. I guess that sounds very Biblical.

I had a chance to go to a private school in New York City, but when I heard all about the racial mix here, I liked that idea. However, I know that I'm compromising my academic career. The private schools offer a more rigorous curriculum. My mom often asks me if I felt I made the right decision. And I answer, "I would have been a totally different kind of person if I had gone to one of those private schools."

The people here seem more real. Had I gone to private school, almost everyone would be white and upper class. They talk the same, they do the same things. That's boring.

The question is, Why should I care about being with people who are different? I don't know the answer to that. I only know there is something decent and good about caring for people who are different from you.

I came here expecting to find a totally integrated student society. I was wrong. As in other racially mixed places, the races only mix superficially. People form their own cliques. The relationship between the whites and the Asians is improving. But the blacks and the Asians? Forget it. It's so sad.

People often stereotype the Asians as the smart people. I do it, too. I say, "Oh, she only got a 95 on that test? But she's Asian. She should have gotten a 100." Afterwards, I realize, wait a minute, she's a human being, she's not Ms. Perfect. I must admit that I resent the fact that most of the Asians refuse to interact with the rest of us. They sit together in the classrooms and eat their lunch together in the lunchroom. When you approach them, they freeze.

CHAPTER **5**

Icebreaker Incident

SPLAT! An ice cube slams into the neck of one of two Chinese students on their way home from school.

"Hey, what's going on?" one boy shouts angrily as the other one wipes the back of his neck.

"Just kidding. Just kidding, man," laughs one of the students walking behind them. The two boys behind, one an African-American and the other an Hispanic, are fooling around, throwing ice from the fruit stands of a Korean market. The Chinese guys don't go along with the fun.

"Damn nigger! Fucking spik!" they grunt.

The laughter stops. Battle lines based on race are quickly drawn. "Fu Manchu! Geek! Chink! Go back to where you came from," the black and Hispanic boys reply.

By the time the four kids reach the Twenty-third Street subway station, fists replace the words. Punching, kicking, jabbing. Books and papers spray across the sidewalk. One of the Chinese students hits the concrete and the African-American jumps on top of him. The other Chinese boy exchanges karate punches with the Hispanic. "Kick him. Get him. Hit'm again," shout the crowd of teenagers who circle around the fighting boys.

A squad car, siren screaming, roars up the avenue. The police officers break up the fight without much difficulty and haul the kids back to the school.

In her office, Dean Barbara Williams, an assistant principal, history teacher, and the adviser to the African-American Club, calms everyone down and listens to the boys' complaints. She offers a simple choice: mediation or suspension. They choose mediation.

Humanities High has a program that enables students to reconcile their differences by means of trained mediators. These mediators come from the student body, the faculty, and the parents.

All four boys involved in the "icebreaker incident" air their grievances and with a little prodding come to an understanding. Before leaving the mediation room, they sign a confidential memo promising that there will be no more fighting and that the incident is closed.

Cut to the lunchroom. Right after mediation one of the Chinese students sits in the "Chinese section" of the lunchroom with a group of friends. As part of their earlier agreement, he spoke with his friends and told them that everything was settled. No one was to bother the other two kids. A group of African-American and Hispanic boys march up to his table and begin to threaten him. "Watch your back, man. We're gonna get you after school."

The Chinese student angrily confronts the original black and Hispanic students, who swear that they don't even know the threatening students. That doesn't make any sense to the Chinese student. In his culture, when people share a common background, they also share common responsibilities. Therefore the black and Hispanic kids are responsible for the new threats.

In a very short time all four students are not only talking about hurting one another, they are talking about bringing in their friends, too. Racial groups begin to line up against racial groups. Very few racial incidents occur in this high school, so the gossip about it is flying.

"This is a spark that could light a bigger fire," says Lynne King, who heads the mediation program at the school. This spark has to be snuffed out fast. A meeting is called with the principal, guidance counselors, deans, and key teachers and students in the school. Everyone needs to know what was happening and everyone has to pitch in.

CHAPTER 6

A Bunch of Chopsticks

The Asian-American Club

THE Asian-American Club is packed with Chinese students, laughing, chatting, giggling, joking, sharing notes and sodas, while looking at photographs, comparing clothes and hair styles.

Mr. Lederman, a math teacher and the adviser to the group, sits on the edge of his desk, talking comfortably with the kids. He steps aside as the no-nonsense president, Yung, calls the meeting to order.

When Mr. Schwartz, a popular biology teacher who also chairs student-association activities, walks into the room, the group quickly switches to polite mode. Yung explains that Mr. Schwartz wants to talk to the club because of the "icebreaker incident."

Yung moves to the side as Mr. Schwartz begins his talk. "Since you represent Asian students, I'd like to know if you are feeling a sense of prejudice against you in this school."

Silence.

Schwartz continues. "Please be open and specific because I need to know what's going on. We must try to put a stop to some of the racial problems."

Everybody looks down. "Don't be afraid to talk. Please. Tell me what's going on. I don't want you to support that stereotypical description that Asian people don't stick up for themselves and are quiet. Please. I heard you yelling before.

"I'd like someone to break the ice and start talking—or I will call on someone." Yung paces back and forth at the side of the room. She is becoming impatient with the other club members.

No one speaks up. "So no one feels any prejudice?"

Lori, who is also a member of the Humane Humanities Club, takes a deep breath and begins to speak.

"In one of my classes I heard someone say, 'Damn, there's so many Chinese people around the school these days.' "

Schwartz nods his head. "That's a fact. There are more Chinese, more Asians, than there have ever been."

Yung says, "I walk around the halls and the kids say, 'Look, Asians around.' When people see us they move to the other side of the hall."

Then the girls begin to relate their frustrations:

"Just because we are shorter than they are."

"They don't beat you up, but they threaten. We're afraid of them. They are bigger than we are."

Another student raises her hand. "At lunch most of the people get in line for their food. When a black student skips the line, the cashier doesn't say anything. But if a Chinese boy skips, she yells, 'Go back to the end of the line.' "

"And other times the blacks give their money to someone else in the front of the line and the lady cashier doesn't say anything. They don't follow the rules. It isn't easy to get to know the blacks," says another female club member.

"They all sit together in the cafeteria."

"Some of us have trouble understanding their English."

"It sounds sad but some blacks feel that they can push a little Asian girl. They just push and walk away. And Asian people do not say anything. We are afraid to. I have been in the hall where people are pushing and an Asian girl got shoved."

Mr. Schwartz looks at her and asks, "Are there any Asians who will fight back?"

"Oh, yes!" shouts Wai, a senior, to much laughter in the room. Yung leans against the ledge of the windowsill and nods in agreement. She is very happy at the outpouring of contributions.

Now that the club has opened up, Schwartz moves the conversation along. "Do you want it to change or are you happy the way it is?"

Lori replies, "I'd like to see some changes."

Mr. Schwartz moves on. "How many of you do homework every night?" All hands go up.

Most of the students in the school assume that the Chinese students are the smartest and will win all the academic awards.

Jenny, the president of the junior class, says, "I don't think the blacks are right when they say that Chinese people tend to be smarter. I think that if you work hard you will get a reward for it. Our parents teach us that. There are a lot of black students who are very intelligent and very smart. I don't know what their parents teach them. When it gets down to it, we really don't understand each other's culture."

Mr. Schwartz asks the group if they would be willing to teach other students about their culture. All the students say that they would participate in such a venture. One girl is dubious. She says, "If they are willing to learn." Everyone laughs.

Yung cautions her constituency, "If we do this, we must be serious. This has to be more than a conversation about sweet and sour pork."

Yung

WHEN we left Hong Kong to come to the United States, my parents told me a lot of bad things about the black people. Robbing and killing and all that stuff. I had to find out by myself if I liked the white people and the Spanish people. My parents didn't tell me about them.

My parents tease me and call me black because I spend all my money and I'm always begging for more. When they want to tease me very badly they say, "You know what? You're going to marry a black person."

Prejudice doesn't go away in a minute. When I was young I believed what my parents told me. Now I know better. I don't have a bad feeling about blacks in my heart. In this school I have black friends. When people tell me that the black people are mean, I say this is not true. There are some black people who are nice and some black people who are nasty, just like Chinese people.

I went to elementary school in Chinatown. I didn't see any stereotyping

there. How could I? Everyone was Chinese. Some of the students were ABCs. That means "American-born Chinese." Others were FOBs. FOB means "fresh off the boat" and it is a bad insult. I didn't feel prejudiced about the FOBs because I was one of them.

In junior high school I found out everything. I realized that some of the white people are mean and vicious towards Chinese people, especially if you don't know how to speak English. When I tried to say something—at that point I had an accent and I could not speak every word correctly—the white students would make fun of me and embarrass me. I did not want to say anything in class anymore. I kept studying and studying and studying—and not talking. Those years I got my best grades, but there was no participation at all. Zero participation.

In my junior high school I learned who my friends were. It didn't matter what color they were. I met my best friend, her name is Sylvia and she's black. She's very honest. She's not like the black people that I had heard about. If I had not gone to that school, I would never learn this. I would still think the same thing as I did when I came from Hong Kong.

In this school, I have to be honest, there are a lot of black people who are really rude, especially to the little girls. I got into an argument with a tall black boy last year. I was walking in the hall and said, "Excuse me," as I passed him. He pushed me. He pushed me in my shoulder. I asked him, "Why are you pushing me?" I didn't want to start a thing with him, so I walked ahead. My friend saw that he was chasing after me so she tripped him. That boy slapped my friend in the head. My friend started crying and I got so pissed off.

"Why do you do that?"

"She tried to trip me," he yelled. He said that he was chasing after me because he didn't like my attitude. Well, I didn't have any attitude problems 'cause I was just walking through the hall.

We all went down to the nice dean, Mrs. Williams. The dean and the elevator man, Lamar, said that he was really a good kid. Not a good kid in the way that he was always studying and stuff. But a good kid who doesn't hurt people.

Mrs. Williams told me that she thought he was trying to hide the fact that he was scared. He recently came from Africa and felt that he had to act tough

Yung

and mean and vicious to others so that people would not pick on him. I felt sorry for him. He came to the United States because he wanted freedom like everybody else. Like me.

Non-Asians think that Asian people are soft and will not talk back. If a non-Asian yells at a Chinese girl, that girl will immediately shut up, try to hide away, or walk away. First of all, we don't know the language that well. I do, but I'm talking in general. Second, there is the culture. Asian people are more in toward themselves. They hide everything in their hearts. You really can't get anything out of them. I'm willing to say what I think because I believe we should have our own rights and we should express our own feelings.

I never talk to my parents. I never tell them where I'm going because they would say, "No, you can't go." If I never tell them, they won't say no and I don't have to sneak out. I know that if I did sneak out, I would be grounded.

I would never talk about sex to my parents. Never! I learned about sex in school in hygiene class. Before I had hygiene class I did not know that a girl has a period. When I was in sixth grade, my teacher told me a little bit about that. So in seventh grade, when I got it, I wasn't that shocked about the blood. And then when I went home, my sister told me more about it. She just told me what to do but she wouldn't tell me why. Maybe she doesn't know. I will teach my children everything. I'm more Americanized.

My family thinks that I'm too American and they don't like it too much. They would like me to be traditional. They believe that I should clean up the whole house. I'm very lazy. I vacuum the house and my mom usually does the rest. I cook the rice, but I don't know how to cook anything else.

I never get bad grades, so that's not a problem for me. Now, I don't even show my parents my report cards because they trust me to get good grades. They trust me about school, but in other stuff, boys, they do not trust me. My mom does not trust me to go to Buffalo University and to live in the dorm. She says I could not take care of myself. I'm going to apply anyway.

In this school, Chinese students do not participate in activities. I do. Part of the reason that they don't is that our parents won't let us go out.

I'm president of the Asian-American Club. The others in the club are always blaming me. "How come we don't do anything in this club . . . ? We don't do anything. . . . We don't have anything to do. . . ." So I get a trip for them and they say, "Yes, no, maybe, I won't." I could say that is what I hate about the Chinese people. They can never make up their mind. There are some people who can, but I haven't found them yet. I personally couldn't make up my mind immediately, either, but I'm trying to.

I went on the retreat that the school ran about stereotyping. There was this girl, Keesa, who is black, and she's the darker kind of black. She has a mean kind of look, also. I was sure that she would be mean, just like my parents told me. I kept away from Keesa because of her physical appearance. But during the retreat we started talking. I realized that she is really nice. In fact, she is very, very nice. We talk to each other now all the time. At the end of the retreat I told her how I used to feel toward her. She said, "Oooooh, do I look mean?" She doesn't look so mean anymore.

The blacks believe that we are more together and more quiet than they are, but that's not true because I know a lot of Chinese people who are very noisy—troublemakers. It's really the same except that our color and our language are different.

At school meetings the only Asians who talk are me and Lori. The other Asians sit there and don't say anything. Even if they are being picked on, they won't say anything. That bothers me. One time I saw a Korean girl in the lunchroom get up to get something. A Spanish guy sat in her seat. The Korean girl returned and said, "Excuse me, can I have my seat back?" And that guy said, "No," and paid no attention to her. I felt so bad. My friend and I were sitting there. We are more the emotional types. So we stood up and shouted, "You're going to get off the seat now!" And he did.

In China there's a saying: "When you're alone, you're weak. When a whole bunch comes together, you're strong. One chopstick can break easily but a bunch of chopsticks is hard to break." That's why we like to stick together. This is what a Chinese philosopher says. I'm not sure who he is, but I know that all the Chinese people have great respect for him.

Wai

I WAS born in Hong Kong and moved here when I was three years old. I went back to see my relatives when I was in junior high school. A lot of my relatives live in the mountains. My Hong Kong family are more traditional than my American family.

My cousins in Hong Kong are very formal. The adults eat first. The children say, "Father, please eat. Mother, please eat. Grandparent, please eat." It is very traditional, very polite. When I have dinner at home or at my cousin's house in Queens, it is informal, casual.

The stuff I do here, I would never dream of doing there. I would never curse in Hong Kong. When I speak Chinese in Hong Kong, I phrase words in a polite way.

I live at the end of Chinatown, on the border of a Jewish community, an Hispanic community, and an African-American community. My father owns a restaurant on Hester Street. I can see three cultures that are different from my own. There are Hispanic and black people who hang out on the streets, just sitting around and talking. When we see each other we never talk. The adults on my block know me, so they leave me alone, but if I go a few blocks away, the people there try to jump me. They aren't looking for money, just a wilding. One time I threw in a few quick punches and started running. I got lucky because I got away from them. I tend to avoid fights.

I went to a public elementary school, then to Catholic school, and now a public school again. The picking started in elementary school. The Spanish kids picked on me. Then the blacks picked on me. The Jewish kids picked on me, too. Everyone picked on me. I'm not sure if the picking had anything to do with prejudice. It could be that I was a strange person when I was young. I wasn't athletic then. I tended to mostly read books—I still do. My family would rather have me stay home and read a book than go out with friends. At least when I am at home they know that I am safe.

When my grandmother came to this country I was always studying in front of her. She felt that if I stayed home, I would be a smart child, but I wouldn't be a child who knew the world. Although she's a very traditional person, she

sees what is happening. She understands that there will be big changes in 1997, when Hong Kong goes back to China. She thought that I should follow my tradition, but I should have knowledge about what is going on in the world, too. She told my parents, "You have to let go of your child sooner or later. There is a big difference between how safe your child is at home and how safe he will be when he leaves the family." They agreed with her. My family balances it out well.

I never knew what the word prejudice meant until I got to junior high school. I heard it on the news. I got tired of hearing it come up over and over again. Everybody says there's prejudice around here, let's do something about it. Sure, you say, but what are you going to do? If a child is taught to hate, he hates. Education helps in a way. Teaching people about different cultures helps.

I'm never around my neighborhood because I'm either in school or at practice with the track team. After school I do not hang out in the streets, I go into my apartment and study. In the summertime I am a teacher's assistant in an Asian day-care center in my neighborhood.

Young kids really don't know what the words prejudice or hatred mean. That's why I like working with them. When they start growing up, they learn about it. And eventually it can turn into a loaded pistol.

It is hard to know when a situation is really racist and when it is not. I have a friend on the soccer team who calls me whitey. And I call him chink. We reverse the roles just for the fun of it. Chink is an old-fashioned word. Once in a while I still hear it. Nowadays we say "FOB" or "ABC." Most Chinese think I'm an ABC, but in reality I'm an FOB. Few people outside the Chinese community know about these terms. They ask, "Why do you always call each other alphabets?"

People think that if you are Chinese you must be a brain. If I'm out with people of other colors, everyone assumes that I, the Chinese person, am the smartest. They assume that the Chinese person always works hardest, always studies the most, and knows everything there is to know about computers. We're supposed to be good at anything that relates to math, physics, or science. Just because I'm Chinese, that doesn't mean I'm super smart. My S.A.T. score proved that I'm not that great in math. I'm better in verbal. It's a lot of assumptions. And for us kids, it is a lot of pressure.

I don't want to fit the stereotype that the Chinese are all brain children. Some people think I'm a brain child, but not my parents, they know better. They see that I'm working hard to get my grades. I struggle through it. Once in a while I wind up on top.

People also assume that anybody who is Chinese is not athletically inclined. They see Chinese people do all those wimpy sports, like table tennis or gymnastics. I'm on the soccer team and I take scuba diving with Mr. Schwartz.

I would be comfortable bringing a non-Asian to the house, but I don't think my parents would like it. They wouldn't say anything, but it is in our tradition not to. My parents make sure that family and school come first. They want me to have a better education than they had. I think they went as far as high school in Hong Kong. They don't want me to have the kind of jobs that they have now because it is really tough.

Even though I'm Christian, on special name days I burn incense and bring food to my ancestors. I give my ancestors clothing. I make paper gold coins and burn them. The tradition says that when our ancestors receive the coins in heaven, the paper turns into real gold. So they have money, food, and clothing in heaven. This is a way that we keep the spirit of our ancestors living. I don't really believe this literally, but I still follow the tradition. I like the symbolism.

I hope to get a job where I can travel. I would like to see other cultures. The Chinese community is my home and always will be my home, but I want to see outside my house. You can't stay within the house all your life.

CHAPTER **7**

"I Used to Be Mad and Now I'm Really Mad"

The African-American Club

THE day after Mr. Schwartz visited the Asian-American Club, he visits the African-American Club. When he enters the room, he hears the same giggly, noisy banter as he heard at the other club. Rasheeda, the president, and Ms. Williams, the club's adviser, are sitting together on the edge of the teacher's desk, talking and laughing loudly. Schwartz joins them.

Rasheeda calls the group to order and explains why Mr. Schwartz has come to speak with them. He thanks her for the intro and begins his spiel. "Yesterday I met with the Asian-American Club, a very big, thriving club. I talked to them because of the ice-throwing incident. I don't want incidents like that to happen again. I'd like to explore a way to resolve the racial tensions that exist."

Mr. Schwartz continues. "Do you feel that there is ethnic tension or racial prejudice in the school? Please be very open. Make believe I'm purple, not white. I represent all students no matter what their color. I want this to be a safe school where you can get a good education and have fun, without racial problems. I'd like to open this up to you guys."

The students are quick to respond. Once again the girls go first. A girl in the front row says, "Asians are so class conscious. I was in the library and a group of Asian girls were sitting nearby. I overheard their conversation. They were ranking the different races. Ours was dead last."

Stephanie, the captain of the volleyball team, stands up and says, "When

I see a Chinese student, the first thing I think of is someone who is smart.'' She waves her hands and twists back into her seat. ''It's a stereotype. I know it.''

Another student adds, ''In math classes the teachers usually put the hard questions to the Chinese students rather than to the black students. The teachers think the Chinese are better in math.''

A dark-skinned Hispanic boy tries to explain why the rest of the school treats the Asian students differently. ''They're always together. When we come near them, they shut up. They always look like they're doing something special and we are not included.''

Another girl says that some Chinese students were surprised to learn that she lived on West 79th Street. ''They think we are all poor and live in the projects.''

A rather large girl calls out that size had a lot to do with the problem. ''Are you saying,'' Mr. Schwartz interrupts, ''that because the Chinese students tend to be smaller, they are more likely to be picked on?'' Club members nod. Size had been a major complaint of the Asian students. ''Does that mean that a small black student will be picked on rather than a slightly taller Chinese student?''

''Absolutely,'' says Lawrence, a tall, good-looking senior, wearing a green workshirt. No one argues with his assessment. He continues. ''I've seen a black kid pick on another black kid just because he was smaller. It had nothing to do with race. It had to do with size.''

Another tall student, Maggie (name changed), leans against the windowsill in the exact position that Yung was in the day before. ''When I see a black guy coming down a dark street, or even in the hall, I get the feeling that this is an aggressive person, I don't want to tangle with this person. I felt that way in the subway station just today. I saw a big black guy coming toward me and I moved away. I really felt terrible about my reaction, especially since I have a brother who is very big. I wonder how it is with him when he's in the subway. My brother wouldn't hurt a fly. Are people afraid of him?''

Mr. Schwartz wants to know if Maggie would feel the same way if the boy in the train station had been white. After a long pause she replies, ''I would check out his body language and the way he was dressed before I made a decision.''

Schwartz continues to ask questions. "Which groups of students do you have the most problems with?"

"Blacks!" shouts a girl in the back of the room, to the laughter of the group.

"Do you mean that?"

"Yes, because if you are black, you are going to hear it from other blacks if you don't act a certain way."

Schwartz wants to know if they've heard other blacks say, "Stop being white."

"Sure!"

Another student mentions that her friends will also say, "Oh, stop being black."

"Which is worse?" the teacher asks.

"Either one."

Mr. Schwartz asks the group if they would be willing to meet with the Asian-American Club and openly discuss these issues.

Maggie says, "Well, I would do it if they would do it, but they won't do it."

"See, that's part of the problem," says Mr. Schwartz. "I think it would be good for the school if we hold a meeting with the two groups and try to remove some barriers."

"Stereotyping is one of the things we've been talking about in this club," Rasheeda says. "Do we need to meet with the Asian Club?"

"It looks like we do," some others reply.

Ms. Williams makes a suggestion. "It would be nice if we can arrange the seating so that we don't have all the African-Americans on one side of the room and the Asian-Americans on the other. I recently spoke with one of the Asian girls, Yung. She said that she was tired of being stereotyped. She was tired of being treated as a non-person. I mention this because that is one thing both groups have in common. Being African-Americans, I'm sure that we can identify with that. We have talked about our feelings of isolation. I have often heard others say that they can't tell one of us from the other. The Asians are experiencing the same thing. Let's look at what we have in common and not dwell on our differences."

Rasheeda

I USED to go to high school near Howard Beach, a white neighborhood in Brooklyn. I was afraid that somebody would call me a nigger. I didn't know what I would do if someone flat-out called me that, a nigger. That kind of racism is indescribable. It is more than scary. I was grateful when my family moved to Manhattan.

In this school we were rehearsing a skit for Ethnic Heritage Day. We were doing an improvisation about two friends who try to break up an interracial couple. I played the girlfriend, and a white guy played my boyfriend. Jeanne (name changed), who is Irish, had to yell, "Get away from that nigger!" At first she couldn't do it. But for the good of the play, she had to. She took a deep breath and shouted out those five awful words: "Get away from that nigger."

When I heard the word hurled at me, I reacted in a way that surprised me. It was not the way that I pictured I would feel. It took about ten seconds before I realized, "Oh, she called me nigger. . . . Oh, my goodness. . . . She did it . . . she called me nigger." Jeanne felt terrible. She kept saying, "I'm so sorry, Rasheeda, I'm so sorry." She told us that she had been fighting with her family all her life because they used words like that.

Hearing that word, actually, finally, at last, was very strange. I felt it physically. Not like a blow or a punch. More like a stab, like a stab in the heart. I wonder if there are words that white people feel offended by, like the way I feel about "nigger"?

I was born in Washington, D.C. My parents had four other children, two girls and two boys. We lived with a group of Muslims who came in all different shades, so I never noticed a person's color. I saw people for who they were.

My father was an Imam, a Muslim preacher. Every midday he went to the mosque to pray. In college, he studied to become a librarian and drove a cab to support his family. My mother used to be a Jehovah's Witness. In the sixties she became a Muslim, too, a Sunni Muslim.

My father died on my parents' anniversary. He was carrying a lot of money on him to buy my mother a present. While he was in his cab, somebody tried to rob him. He wouldn't give up the money, so they shot him in the left

side of his neck and the right side of his stomach. That's the official version.

There's another version that I think is probably more accurate. Some political people came, put him in his cab, had him lie down on the floor in a prayer position, and shot him. I heard that they did it to another Imam the same way, using the same ammo.

Right after my father was killed, my mother moved us all to her mother's house in New York. Even though I was only five, I knew what was going on. I loved my father. My little sister was still in my mother's womb. She never saw him. My brothers went into shock. After the shooting, they did poorly in school.

My grandmother didn't like my mother's conversion to Islam. We wore head scarves like the Muslims wear. My grandmother would yell, "Take those rags off your heads."

I would say, "Grandma, you shouldn't say that."

She once told me, "Jesus was God's son."

"He wasn't," I shouted. "He was a prophet of God." I had a strong belief.

When I lived in D.C., all the kids were the same, be they Puerto Rican or black. On my block there were even a few white kids and some Chinese. After we moved to New York, I noticed that people treated me differently because I was black and a Muslim. For example, my first day in first grade, I wore my head wrap. A kid came up to me and said, "You an alien." Then he sang, "Come back to Jamaica. . . ."

"What you saying that for?" I demanded.

" 'Cause you black. Blacks live in Jamaica." I started crying. Then I threw an apple at him.

A lot of Puerto Ricans think that I'm Jamaican because I have dark skin. The only black people my Hispanic neighbors seemed to remember are the ones on TV's "Come back to Jamaica" commercials. That's why they thought I was Jamaican.

My mother is a drug counselor. She works for the New York City Board of Education. I love my mother. Self-worth has a lot to do with how you live your life, how you feel about yourself. She has taught me to be proud of who I am ever since I was a child.

We live with my grandmother. Some of my mother's brothers and sisters are

Rasheeda

Muslims and some are Jehovah's Witnesses. We learned to live with two religions in our family. This may sound like a stereotype, but the Muslims have tons of kids and the Jehovah's Witnesses have one or two kids. I think my grandmother favors the Jehovah's Witnesses.

Last summer I went to Egypt with the International Youth Leadership Institute. Everyone was black or Hispanic in our group. We visited the different temples and palaces for three weeks.

In Egypt I saw people who looked black, just like me. That made my trip. When I was in elementary and junior high school, we studied all about Egypt. I thought I knew everything there was to know about Nefertiti. None of our books and none of my teachers ever said that Nefertiti was black. I always wondered that since Egypt was in Africa, how come the people weren't black? Then, I saw the temple walls. I saw Cleopatra. She had braids like me! And she had hair like me! That blew me away. Now all I do is think about Egypt.

There was one temple where there was still color paint on the drawings. All the people in the pictures were really dark. I was stunned. Then I got mad. I used to be mad, but now I'm really mad. In my social studies books I saw only one paragraph devoted to black people. I knew there was more to us than that.

It is important for me to know more about my heritage. I don't know why I feel this way, but I do. I really do. A few weeks ago I went to a family get-together. My grandmother went through our whole heritage. It was very complicated. Her father's people, my great-grandfather, came from Ireland. His name was Kennedy. He was a white Irishman. My grandmother says that there is a Kennedy family in South Carolina, who is white, and attends our family reunions and everything. They recognize that we are cousins.

My great-great-grandmother was a Black Foot Indian. Somebody must have been a slave in there somewhere because her son, who was my other grandmother's father, turned out colored. Negro. Black. African-American.

I'm very proud of what I am, but there are some things about African-Americans that bother me. I don't like it when light-skinned African-Americans act like they are better than everyone else. Many do. Even in this school, where you would never expect a thing like that. There are girls in this school who think they are better than anyone else just because they have light skin.

Because I'm the president of the African-American Club, I got complaints from some white students when we put up black-power posters during Black History Month. The word power has a different connotation when you say "black power" from when you say "white power." Black power means the power to do what you want to do: the power to be a congressman, the power to be President. It also means the power to be able to feed your family and buy the clothes you need to keep you warm. Kids wear black-power T-shirts because they are trying to build up the power that has been stripped away.

To me, a white-power T-shirt is the reverse of black power. It means that whites want even more power to continue to put down the black people. When I think of white power, I think of the power to make black people slaves: to keep us down even longer under the white man's big old heavy shoes.

Lawrence

I WAS walking down the street and this Chinese man was coming towards me shouting terrible things about black people. I think he was drunk. As I approached him, he looked at me as if he was in shock. He screamed, "Oh, my God, look at this guy, he's half black and he's half white! We can't save him now! Too late, man, you have black in you!" I laughed so hard. It was pretty foolish.

Because I have very light skin, a lot of people think I'm half and half. I don't want to sound prejudiced, but I consider myself black. When I was younger, my hair was straight and blond. I wanted it to be crinkly, like the black people. Then, when my hair got more crinkly, I wanted it to be straight again.

I used to hang out with a lot of hoodlums, the baggy-pants kids who like to cause trouble. My friends were beating on other people just because they were different. To be truthful, I sometimes did it too.

In the ninth grade I changed completely. My fifteen-year-old brother suddenly had a heart attack and passed away. I discovered what it is like to feel pain, real pain. I questioned why I would want to hurt another person just because he looked different. Then I met a guy who was white and we started hanging out together. I found that we had a lot in common.

Sometimes my friends tease me. They call me "Vanilla Ice," the white rapper. They say I am a walking "what?" I laugh with them. I don't really react to insults. I guess you just have to love yourself.

P.S. The African-American and Asian-American clubs did eventually attend a meeting sponsored by the Humane Humanities Club. It was an open, raucous, no-holds-barred meeting. One concrete aftermath was a three-day retreat in upstate New York where students and teachers discussed racism, sexism, and homophobia. After the retreat the students reported that they had a greater sensitivity about racism, their most heated arguments centered around sexism, and some still could not overcome their homophobia.

Lawrence

CHAPTER 8

If Your Best Friend Is Gay

Health-Education Class

STEVE Carrillo walks into Mr. Howort's fifth-period health-ed class. Steve's long, wavy, brown hair, sensual lips, and Tom Cruise-like eyes give him rank as the best-looking boy in the school. Steve looks toward the board where the day's "aim" is prominently displayed: homosexuality.

"Oh, man," he complains, slapping his side. "I was all prepared to talk about masturbation." He takes his seat next to Paul, a tall, lanky, good-looking fellow with creamy chocolate skin, close-cropped hair, and a wicked sense of humor.

"You been practicing?" he laughs.

"Yeah, man," replies Steve. "I got a master's degree in masturbation." They high-five, low-five, and every-way-you-can-five each other until Mr. Howort calls the class to order.

The seats in Mr. Howort's class are arranged in a large circle. Graffiti on the side chalkboard read: *The lover and the lovette . . . It's totally cool dude . . . Emily and Raheen . . . Love . . . Herb and Sweetness.* Mr. Howort sits with the class, not behind a desk. He starts his lesson by asking the students to define what qualities go into being a best friend. As the group begins calling out adjectives, Ara, the vice president of the school, writes them on the chalkboard.

The class calls out "friendship" words: "Loyal." "Faithful." "Trustworthy." "Open-minded." "Understanding." "Will never leave you. . . ."

Then the teacher asks the class, "Who decides who will be your best friend?"

Paul becomes outraged at the notion that anyone would have the audacity to tell him with whom to be friends. In fact, all the students vehemently insist that they choose their own friends.

The teacher leans forward on his elbows and folds his hands under his chin. Very slowly he poses his hypothetical situation: "Let's say that your very best friend says, 'I have to tell you something that is very important.' And then your best friend tells you that he or she is a homosexual. (Pregnant pause) I would like you to write down on a piece of paper what questions you would ask him or her about homosexuality." Notebooks open and the writing begins.

After about five minutes the teacher adds another question to the assignment. "Now write what effect this revelation will have on your friendship?"

Once the class is finished writing, they pass their questions to the teacher, who begins to read them out loud, without identifying the authors. Some of the students' questions are:

"What is it like to be sexual with another person, especially since I'm not? . . . How do you feel? . . . How did you think I'd react? . . . I'd ask if she had homosexual feeling toward me? . . . Are you bisexual? . . . Do your parents know? . . . Why are you a homosexual?"

As Howort reads their questions, he answers the physiological and logistical questions, gives statistics, and breaks down stereotypic myths. All the while he brings up ethical problems for the class to consider and debate.

"Here's an interesting question," Howort says. " 'Are you sexually active?' This implies that a person can be a homosexual and not engage in any homosexual acts. Do you think that's possible?"

"Yeah," shouts Ara, and all the boys look at her and smirk. Ara defends her position with aplomb. "If I'm attracted to a guy, that doesn't mean that I'm going to sleep with him. I can just think he's cute."

"Right," the teacher agrees. "You do not have to be sexually active to feel very strongly attracted to someone of your own sex."

An Hispanic girl says, "I think that homosexuality is a sin, because that's what I learned in church."

Another boy raises his hand. "Some religions do not consider it as a sin."

Mr. Howort does not want the discussion to be sidetracked to a religious debate. So he moves the conversation along by reading another question. "Do your parents know?" He says that four of the five gay students in the graduate

class that he attended at Brooklyn College told their parents that they were gay. And they all said that their parents were disappointed, but they still loved them.

Steve calls out, "That wasn't exactly an encouragement."

"No. It was reality," replies the teacher. "I think that most parents eventually accept it."

Howort asks how many people tell their parents that they are heterosexually active. Paul says that he would tell his father. The other boys would not. Nelsa, an Hispanic junior, says that where sex is concerned, there is a big barrier between parents and kids.

David, an Irish-American, adds, "You learn bad things about gays at home, though. My parents told me that they could accept anything but that. If I told my parents that I was gay, it would be their worst nightmare. They impose their views on me."

"I heard that when some people say that a person is gay, they just assume that the gay is going to attack them, and I think that is wrong," says Nelsa. "They are people, not freaks."

The biggest fear the kids say they have about sex is the idea that someone could force himself on them. Rape. People often assume that a gay person will come after them. Therefore, a gay person is to be feared. The teacher wants to know, "Who does most rapes?"

"Sick straight men," Ara says pointedly, and everyone agrees.

Mr. Howort says, "You have more to fear from the drunken straight guy at a party than from someone who is gay. Most sexual crimes are by men against women, not women against women or men against men."

The teacher asks if everybody agrees with what has been said so far. When everyone nods in the affirmative, the class moves on.

At this point Howort brings forward a historical example. "The Puritans had an interesting view of sex. The only kind of sex allowed was intercourse between married people with the man on top of the woman. No other way."

"How would they know what the couple was doing?" asks the Hispanic churchgoing girl.

"How would they know?" the teacher replies. "Imagine this: You have a community of very religious people who have a strong belief about this prac-

Mr. Howort

tice. Then, one night, a husband says to his wife, 'Did you ever think about trying a different position?' The wife goes screaming out of the house to the leaders of the group. 'He's possessed by the devil!' The wife would think she was married to an immoral man. A pervert. He would be exposed and punished. My point is that the Puritans thought that the very sexual activities that we take for granted are the work of the devil."

The students are fascinated and want to know more. "What else? What else?"

"Another example is the ancient Greeks. It was normal for the men to have homosexual activity."

"The ancient Greeks were gay?" asks Paul, his eyes practically popping out of their sockets.

"Yeah. Often among privileged free males in Greek society, adolescent boys would be courted by older men who saw the boys as representatives of ideal beauty. It was a normal step in growing up to have an older man as a mentor and sometimes as a sexual partner. As soon as the boy's beard began to grow, the relationship usually ended and the young man went on to heterosexual relationships. When he himself became older, he became a mentor to adolescent boys. So we can see that the issue about what is normal and what is abnormal depends on the view of society."

Once the teacher moves on to the question about what effect the friend's homosexuality would have on their relationship, the responses are mixed. "If my best friend was gay, that would have no effect on me because I'd love her no matter what. Besides, she trusted me enough to tell me . . . I would feel awkward when talking about the opposite sex . . . I would be frightened." Howort stops reading to tell the class that the reason he is holding this discussion is so that people won't be quite so threatened and frightened.

One male student is worried about what his other friends might think if they found out he has a gay friend.

"And what would they think?" asks Howort.

"They might think the gay guy would try something with us, stuff like that. Our friendship would have to end."

"You would really rather give up the friendship?" the teacher asks.

"Right."

Paul interrupts, "Read mine. . . ."

"We would remain friends because I wouldn't want to betray him. But if the peer pressure got too bad for either of us, like if his gay friends tried to convert me or my friends shut me out, then we would probably drift apart." Paul has added, in parentheses, "I will admit that I do have a small prejudice against gay people, but I try to hide it."

The issue of peer pressure is an important one. Many students freely admit that they would give up the friend rather than face the stigma of hanging out with a gay person.

Paul justifies his position by suggesting that you are always going to have friends. "A person can't base his life on one friend."

"Wait a minute. I have a lot of friends who ask why I hang out with black kids," argues Ara. "Should I give up my friends because they are black?"

Paul, who is black, jumps out of his seat. "If a straight person hangs around with a gay person, he might turn gay."

Ara finds his reasoning outrageous. "Does it follow that if I hang out with my black friends, I'll turn black?"

Mr. Howort reminds the students that they said that *they* decided who their friends were going to be. Have they come to a different conclusion? "Who really decides?" the teacher asks.

"Society!" answers Ara triumphantly, while eyeing Paul.

It appears that peer pressure may force some students, especially the males, to give up a friendship. The teacher draws a conclusion. "You are giving up a real friend either because of unreal fears or because of what other people may think." He points to the chalkboard, where *loyal, open-minded, trustworthy,* etc., are boldly written. "What about those . . . ?"

The bell rings. The lesson is finished.

CHAPTER **9**

Loving a Woman

Rachel (Name Changed)

PEOPLE use terms like faggot and dyke without really understanding what they are saying. When someone uses the term faggot, I get so upset, I want to throw up. Often, they aren't even saying it to someone who they think is a homosexual. They just say it to a friend who did something stupid. People don't know the history of the words that they use. They don't know that a faggot was a bundle of sticks that was used to burn homosexuals. They don't realize how much pain another person might feel when they use that word.

In classrooms, I've heard some teachers use the words homo, faggot, and dyke in casual conversation. They use it to dis somebody, to insult somebody. Teachers know what they're doing when they say those words. They're older, they gotta know. When a person in authority uses words like that, he's giving kids permission to use them, too. That promotes homophobia and it promotes gay bashing.

There is one kid in this school who goes gay bashing on Saturday nights. That really makes me want to throw up. When he bragged to me about it, I said, "That's sick. I can't believe you did that."

He seemed shocked by my reaction. He said, "Well, I just had to let off some steam."

I couldn't let it pass. I said, "Don't you know that is totally unacceptable behavior? Morally, you should feel like shit."

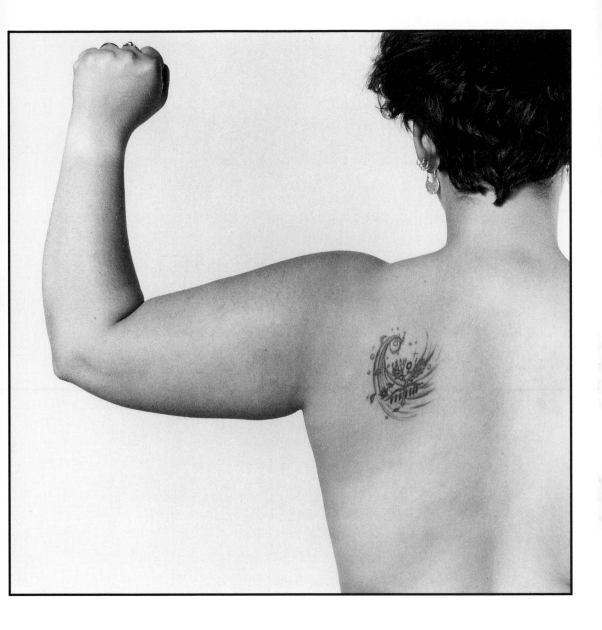

"Rachel"

In my current events classes I often brought up sexism and homophobia because that was what I think about. After a while I noticed that people were nudging me in the hall. I felt threatened.

I became afraid about what would happen if my classmates found out that I was gay. I was afraid of physical violence. I didn't want to be the token dyke at the school. I didn't want to be constantly defending myself. And I certainly didn't want to become an angry person because I was always defending myself.

Lesbians are very interested in the safety of women. It's very important for me to feel strong and safe. I try to give that to other women, all other women.

Luckily, the threats didn't make me question who I am. For me, the issues never have been, "Am I? Is it okay? Is it not okay?" I always felt that whatever my choice, it would be okay. I think that I'm a minority among gay teenagers in that respect.

I get support from my family. That, too, is very rare. When I was thirteen I told my parents how I was feeling. I gave them literature about how to be supportive of gay teenagers. A year later, when I was fourteen, we were on a vacation in Europe. I'll never forget the scene: we were in a café having breakfast. The conversation turned to love. I told them that I had fallen in love—with a woman. It felt so much better to say the words.

My father dropped his fork and my mother just sat there. I think my mother knew all along. My father is very interested in my sister and me. He loves us very, very much. He likes to know everything that is going on in my life. He asked blunt questions. "What do you do? Physically? Sexually?" At that point I hadn't done anything.

The first time I introduced him to a woman whom I was involved with, he asked me if I slept with her. "Would you ask me that if I was involved with a man?" I asked.

He said that he knew what a man and a woman did. I didn't tell him, but I wouldn't tell him about a boyfriend either. That's none of his business. We did talk about the emotional part, though.

In 1988 I had my first big crush. It was over a camp counselor who I knew was a lesbian. I figured out that I had a crush on her because I was feeling the same kind of attraction that I had previously felt about guys. I went through all the typical first-love stages. I constantly walked past her, worked where she worked, played silly songs on the guitar, and wrote poems. I guess it was puppy love, but it felt so strong. Eventually I told her about it. She was twenty-three and I was sixteen. We never had a relationship.

I worry about telling my straight friends that I am gay. What will they think of me? That's a form of homophobia. Perhaps that's why I like to be with other gay people. I like that a lot. I love gay men. I think they are awesome.

At my camp, I spoke with another counselor who I knew was gay. I asked, "Are there other gay campers?" It turned out that there were and we formed a support group where we could talk about everything. One day we talked about our fears in coming out. Another day we giggled about how to make out.

The following year we formed the group again and that was where I met my first real relationship, Julie (name changed). We'd been friends for five years. I knew what I felt, but I didn't know what she was feeling. When Julie told me that she was attracted to me, I was completely blown away. Julie looked like a model. She's very beautiful. She's a dancer. I thought that there was no way she would have any feeling for me. Although I tried not to, I still believed in the homophobic bullshit that lesbians are a certain stereotype. Heavy. Masculine. Aggressive. Butch.

We always sat next to one another during staff meetings. During one meeting we started writing little doodly notes to each other and we got into silly innuendos about sex. Then she wrote that she had to talk to me about something and I wrote back, "Great, I have to talk to you, too."

After the meeting we started talking about how we were feeling very out of synch with the rest of the group. Julie started to cry. "What's wrong?" I asked.

"Rachel, I'm attracted to you."

I didn't know what to say. "I–I–I'm attracted to you, too." By this time we were both crying, "Oh, my God, I can't believe this is happening." We were excited and scared and wondering what came next.

It took us about three weeks to get comfortable with each other. The whole thing was very scary. Having an idea that it was okay to be attracted to women is one thing. Getting involved with a woman is quite another. All my fears came back, the homophobia, the stereotypes, the stigmas.

Once I was in the relationship, it became more and more important to me to let people know that it really is a part of me. We told the camp community. One of the campers started making comments about us. He said that with Julie's looks there was no way she could be a lesbian. She was definitely bisexual. "But," he added, "Rachel definitely is a lesbian." That totally pissed me off. I hadn't decided what I was, and yet here was this little shit telling everyone else what I was.

Julie and I were together a month and a half into the summer. Everything was great. Then she started hanging out with a male counselor. A number of times I asked her what was going on. Why was she hanging out with him and not with me? She would only admit that they were friends.

A few weeks later I found out that Julie had fallen in love with the counselor and was having a relationship with him. We didn't officially break up. We just stopped talking. It broke my heart.

All my homophobia returned. "I'm overweight. I'm ugly. That's why people see me as a lesbian. I shouldn't be feeling these things." Intellectually, I never believed any of that junk. That was completely irrational. I was contradicting myself right and left. I was confident about my role as a woman loving a woman but I couldn't come out and define myself as a lesbian.

When I returned to school everything was different. I felt it was important for me to come out to my friends here. I ended up telling my five closest friends. Four of us are still friends. My fifth friend turned out to be homophobic and we drifted apart.

I met my new girlfriend, Jane, at camp last summer. When she told me that she had a crush on me, I was apprehensive. She is a very strong-looking woman. I was sure that she was a very experienced lesbian. She seemed very aggressive.

She's twenty-three, an older woman. It was very flattering, but it was also "YIKES!!!!" It turned out that she only came out to herself when she was nineteen. That amazed me because I had been out to myself since I was nine. She was as afraid about approaching me as I was afraid about being approached. We became involved eight months ago.

Jane is staunch in her conviction that she's a lesbian. She says, "That's my title. That's what you call me." I can't do that yet. Anyway, I don't like titles. In fact I can't stand them. What happens if I become attracted to a man? I have been.

Some people say that lesbians simply cannot get a man. That's not what it's about at all. Loving a woman is just that: loving another woman.

CHAPTER 10

"I'm an Illusion"

In the Auditorium

MR. Steward, the director, is conducting the chorus. Tracy, who often sings a solo during a choir program, stands out in the crowd. He is tall, lean, and handsome, with dazzling doe-shaped eyes and an infectious smile.

After the song, Mr. Steward says there will be a five-minute break. One of the female singers marches over to Tracy.

She says, "Tracy, you shouldn't try to be a woman. The other girls give you respect because you get loud in the cafeteria. I dislike everything you do, and you'll never get any respect from me. In fact, I can't stand you."

Tracy is a very hard person to hurt. Years ago he built a thick shell around himself as a protection from name calling. Usually it is the boys who taunt Tracy and the girls who befriend him. This unexpected outburst throws him off balance. Tracy says, "The more people call me names, the more it rolls off my back. But for some reason this really hit me hard."

Tracy remains imperially aloof until it is time to resume singing. After a few minutes he raises his hand and asks to go to the bathroom. On the way to the boys' bathroom, tears are rolling.

Later, Tracy says, "I went to the bathroom and cried. I was alone in the bathroom, so nobody knew about it. I want the world to see that I'm strong. When I'm by myself, I can be weak.

"It was the first time in a long time that anyone said something that actually hurt me. I've been called a faggot by my grandmother, but she only says that when she's highly upset."

Tracy

'M one of those loud, flamboyant homos, as my mother would say. I get loud or flamboyant only when it is necessary, which is all the time. Take, for example, the day I was sitting on a train and a guy screamed out "faggot" just by looking at me. He was a dark-skinned guy with a whole bunch of gold teeth and some heavy gold around his neck. He was trying to impress the girls on the train. He was young, about eighteen or nineteen.

Now, my mother always told me that you don't have to be loud and flamboyant to be noticed. One homo knows another homo, regardless of whether you're loud or not. You always know your own kind.

So when the guy pointed at me and said, "faggot," and then said, "homo," I remembered what my mother taught me, and I was ready to answer back. I said, "We all know what you are, because you slept with me last night. Or was that your little brother?"

All the people on the train looked at me, and then looked at him, and their eyeballs nearly jumped out of their sockets. The guy got up and moved to the next car. I thought he would punch me out, but he didn't. I was surprised. Homophobic people are so insecure.

Most people don't understand the flamboyant homos. It's fun to be flamboyant. A friend said, "Homosexuals lead exciting lives." And that's true, especially if you are flamboyant. You never know what you are going to do until you do it. Like last month. I had no idea that I was going to cut all my hair off. I went to bed. Then, in the middle of the night, I woke up and thought, "I don't want hair anymore." So I just cut it all off. When I make my changes, I make them *big* and I make them known.

The reason why I dress up like a woman is for the adventure. I put on a skirt and go on the train just to see if I'm so good-looking that a man can't tell that I'm a boy. It's worked many times. I've even gone to school parties when boys

from the school didn't know who I was. I have the phone number of a boy who actually thought I was a real girl. I never told the guy it was me. That was an adventure.

Dressing like a girl makes me feel more real, more womanlike. It's actually fun, it really is. Girls are allowed to dress like men, but boys aren't supposed to dress like women. Girls are allowed to play with cars and dolls. And guys aren't allowed to play with dolls, only cars. It's not normal. Why can't everybody be equal?

The other day I was on the bus and a woman came over to me. She said, "Excuse me, I don't want to be rude, but on one hand you look like a female and on the other hand you look like a male. Which are you?" I told her, "I'm not a man or a woman. I'm an illusion."

Flamboyants are careful about color coordination. Everything has to be exact, right down to our sneakers. Next Friday night I'm planning to wear brown and black. Everything must match. That's one of the rules of being flamboyant.

I have eight sisters and five brothers. Different mothers, same father. Busy dad. I'm fifth from the bottom. My father is a bus driver. And my mother is a housewife.

I realized that I was gay when I was twelve. I was not attracted to women. Only boys. A lot of people think that I'm gay because I was an overprotected child. I was brought up like a girl. I had to call home every other hour when I went out on Saturday nights.

My strict parents didn't make me gay. Actually, what made me gay is me. I felt gay. I thought gay. For example, I have never had a fight in my life. I try to fight, but I can't. Either my sisters defend me or my mother defends me.

The worst thing a parent wants to hear about a child is that he or she is gay. But it is important that the child tell the parent before somebody else does. My parents are nice, homey people. My dad says that it really doesn't matter if I'm a homosexual or a heterosexual, just so long as I'm something. I'd rather be a homosexual than a crackhead. Anybody would take that choice.

My father has one problem about my being gay. He doesn't want me to act like a girl around my little brother. He feels that what I do will rub off on him. My brother wants to do everything that I do. He's very feminine, too.

We don't have any macho teachers here. It's kind of laid-back. There are several homosexual male teachers in this school.

Being gay never bothered me. When people politely ask me questions, I love to answer them. Some girls ask me if I'm the man or the woman in the relationship. I tell them, "I'm the girl."

Safer sex is constantly bashed through my head by my father. I think that everybody should have safer sex, not just homos. Girls should have safer sex with guys. I know a girl who actually thinks that after sex you should jump up and down, and the sperm will leave the body, and you won't get pregnant. And they say I'm weird!

CHAPTER 11

Yuppies, Gangsters, & Nerds

Wendy & Jenny

AT the end of another school day, a number of students, all female, remain in the S.A. office to plan for the senior Student Association election. Jenny is making a run for senior president, and her best friend, Wendy, is her running mate. Their opponents are Ben, the Cuban-Greek-American who is in Humane Humanities Club, and his running mate, Pharaoh, a popular African-American who is a star basketball player.

"We're in big trouble," groans Wendy, every time Ben's or Pharaoh's name is mentioned.

Jenny says, "Last year I won because there are a lot of Chinese-Americans in my class. I'd like to say that I won because I gave a very good speech. Everyone told me how terrific it was. But I'm pretty sure it was because I ran against two other girls, one black and the other Korean. The Chinese kids voted for me because I'm Chinese, even though I don't hang out with them much. Besides, the Chinese kids don't like the Koreans."

Wendy says that she doesn't like the Koreans much, either. "They look down on Chinese people because we don't have as much money as they have. They think that we're not as rich and we're not as classy."

Jenny looks puzzled. "I don't believe you really think that."

Wendy amends her evaluation. "If I meet an individual Korean, I don't hate her. I dislike the stereotypical things about her. Once I get past that, it's okay."

"I think Wendy is a man-hater," says Jenny.

"I'm a feminist," corrects Wendy. "A feminist is someone who wants equal rights for women."

Jenny says, "I want women to have more power. It is unfair that women get raped and men don't. Why should we be scared when we walk down the street at night? Men aren't scared."

Wendy says, "We get cramps every month. And we get fat and ugly when we have babies. We're against that."

"I would say that we are against men," muses Jenny in a dreamy voice.

"They are so immature," reports Wendy.

"It has been proven scientifically that women develop earlier and faster."

"They think differently. Men don't express themselves as openly as we do."

"They keep their feelings inside."

"And," says Wendy, "they compare the size of their you-know-what."

Jenny often looks for logical reasons to back up her statements. "Some men will talk about their feelings, but more women do than men. I think it all has to do with the way they were raised. Their fathers taught them that they should never show pain. They should never show any emotions because that is a sign of weakness. I don't feel pity or disdain for men. They are people, too."

Wendy says, "Right now I think I will never get married and never have kids."

Jenny is less militant. "I don't have a boyfriend right now, but sooner or later I will get married. I think it would be nice to have a kid growing up who looks just like me. I wouldn't like to be in a place where everyone was Chinese, either. It isn't realistic. I like being in a multicultural environment," Jenny continues without missing a beat.

She explains that her mother has never been out of Chinatown in her entire life. She describes her mother as fearful about things she doesn't know. "She speaks very little English. She is a sensitive and delicate person who stays home and takes care of seven kids." Perhaps that is why Wendy is quick to say, "Raising a kid is a pain."

Although Wendy insists that she is not interested in men, she is curious about interracial dating. She says, "Chinese families are becoming a little more accepting when it comes to dating white guys. But when a Chinese family sees one of their own with a black guy, they shake their heads, as if to say, 'You

should be ashamed of yourself.' It's all in the look! All Chinese kids know that look. Yet, black families don't like Asian women dating their guys either. They want to preserve their culture just as much as the Chinese do."

"Some people go out with other races because it is the 'in' thing to do," adds Jenny. "Black guys are the most aggressive. One guy on the train walked up to me and asked me out, right then and there. I didn't even know him."

Both young women admit that Chinese guys can be a problem. They say that they are less aggressive than white, black, or Hispanic guys. "I've known one Chinese guy for a year and a half. He smiles at me in class, but he won't say anything unless I speak first. Chinese guys don't ask you out. They talk to you in class."

Wendy explains that Chinese teenagers are easily classified. "There are some who want to be white. I know some Asians who aren't proud of their heritage. They dress like yuppies and talk like 'Valley girls.' "

According to Wendy and Jenny, there are three types of Chinese guys: the yuppies, the gangsters, and the nerds. "The gangsters have spiked hair and wear black clothes. The top part of their pants is baggy and the legs are tight. They wear shoes with no socks, hang out with their own race, and only talk Chinese. They used to carry beepers, but Mrs. Jarvis outlawed them in the school. They run around with Chinese girls who have spiked hair and wear black, too. They won't talk to the girls who wear color. The girls who dress in color, pastels, won't talk to the ones in black because they are afraid. The gangsters scare them.

"The yuppies wear stylish, brand-name clothes. They don't hang out with their own race. They hang out with the whites. They have the latest hair styles, hundred-dollar shoes, and million-dollar faces. Everything has to be picture-perfect. They flaunt what they have. The guys dress in a preppie-yuppie style. They are clean-cut, all-American types. The yuppies walk around with larger-than-life attitudes. The girls are JAPS, Jewish-American Princesses. Just like the Koreans.

"Both the gangsters and the yuppies care about the way they act, walk, talk, and look. They hide the fact that they get good grades or else they will be perceived as nerds.

"The nerds make up the majority of the community. They are obsessed with

Wendy and Jenny

studying. Very few date. They don't care about fashion and aren't concerned about popularity. They want good grades and think the other two groups are superficial.

"Gangster guys date gangster girls, and the yuppie guys date yuppie girls, and the nerds date no one at all."

CHAPTER **12**

"Hang the Woman"

Mr. Hirsch's English Class

A ROACH!" screams Gina. Everyone jumps out of their seats. "Don't kill it! Don't kill it! It's Gregor!"

Gregor is the protagonist in Kafka's "Metamorphosis," a story about a man who wakes up one morning to find himself changed into a roach. It was the class's previous reading assignment.

Mr. Hirsch, who had been writing on the chalkboard, turns around. With twinkling eyes, he says forebodingly, "Maybe it's a student who didn't come to class today."

"It's Zuzu!" shouts Maggie, the tall black student who is also in the African-American Club. "He woke up alienated and isolated and became a bug."

Zuzu races into classroom, hands the teacher a note, and apologizes for being late. "Oh, hi, Gregor, glad you decided to return," says Gina, as Zuzu goes to his seat. He looks at her quizzically. The circle of boys who sit around Zuzu explain Gina's remark. Zuzu throws his head back and laughs heartily.

Zuzu is a tall, handsome, Lebanese-American who has a penchant for turtleneck sweaters and chino pants. He is known as the student who makes the most opinionated, argumentative, extreme statements in the entire school. Usually, everyone in class disagrees with something Zuzu says, especially when it comes to politics and religion. Although he will recognize an occasional inconsistency, he generally holds to his convictions with considerable self-confidence.

Mr. Hirsch's English class

Besides the imaginative curriculum, this English course is particularly interesting because the students come from many different ethnic backgrounds. Mr. Hirsch encourages them to bring their own personal, cultural experiences and social ideals to the group. There is a nonthreatening climate in the classroom, but frank discussions are not without a price. Even though the classroom conversations are vastly enriched, there are times when the discussion becomes extremely hot. Sometimes the planned lesson gets lost along the way.

The students, a combination of juniors and seniors, argue, challenge, debate, reflect, and state passionate opinions (however outrageous some of them may be) with little self-consciousness. Humor goes a long way to defuse touchy situations. There is one exception. In this mixed class, the students never criticize anyone's race. But everything else is fair game, especially sexism and homophobia. For some unexplained reason these two subjects usually go hand in hand. Whenever one is brought up, the other is sure to follow. Today's lesson is no exception.

This week the class has been reading a Brazilian short story by Rachel de Queiroz called "Metonymy, or the Husband's Revenge." It is about a husband who finds letters from his wife's lover. The husband doesn't kill his wife or her lover, but rather kills the mailman who delivered the incriminating information. Today's discussion revolves around the husband's action and his subsequent punishment.

"If I was the husband, I definitely would kill the lover," says Anthony, a junior in the second row. "And I'd probably kill the wife, too, because she could do that again to somebody else's husband."

"Ayah," grunt a number of students in the room.

Zuzu gives what he considers a practical assessment of Anthony's decision. "You can only be punished for one murder. Right? If you're going to get the chair, you may as well do it for two people." The entire class begins laughing. Laughter doesn't faze Zuzu one bit.

Whenever Zuzu makes a comment, the class automatically looks to Laura for a response. Laura, a senior of Romanian-Jewish heritage, sits front row, center. She is the one person who can take Zuzu on. Her early school years spent at a yeshiva, an Orthodox Jewish private school, taught her the fine art of debate. The entire class, including Zuzu, recognizes Laura's exceptional intellect. Although Laura is quick to speak out on subjects that are important to her, she recently resolved not to become so emotional in class and to keep her mouth shut no matter what Zuzu says.

Noticing that Laura has remained silent, Denise, an Hispanic girl who rarely volunteers, takes the lead. "Whenever a girl cheats on a guy, the guy always wants to go and kill the other guy. Take it out on the girlfriend, not the other guy."

Gabe, a stocky boy in a red University of Nevada T-shirt, beige Bermuda shorts, white sneakers, isn't buying it. "I wouldn't kill the mailman. If I loved my wife, I'd give her another chance," he says calmly. "But the lover would get it."

"What would you prove by killing the lover?" asks Gina. "They both had a part in the affair. Why should you kill the lover while the other one goes free? How do you know that she won't go out and do the same thing?"

Both Laura and Mr. Hirsch are surprised that the young women in the class seem to favor punishment for the woman while a male, Gabe, does not.

Gabe gets angry. He jumps out of his seat. "Gabe, Gabe, Gabe, hang on. . . ." the teacher says. Hirsch turns toward Gina. "Gina, if you could make a final judgment, what would you do?"

"I would punish the husband because he killed the mailman. I would also punish the wife because she had an affair."

"What would be the appropriate punishment for the husband? For the wife?"

Gina is prudent. "I would put the husband in jail. The wife, no, I would make her feel ashamed, embarrassed."

Zuzu, who is usually unnervingly calm and collected when he speaks, is becoming agitated as he listens to his classmates. He says, "The mailman should never have been punished in any way. He was just doing his job. The husband should be hung. Anybody who kills has to die, except in cases of self-defense and accidents." The class becomes hysterical.

Hirsch asks, "What if you are negligent? What if you are at a party, and you do a little drinking, and you drive your car, and you kill somebody?"

"Hang'm," says Zuzu. "Hang the wife, too. When a woman takes an oath of marriage, she is making a commitment to be loyal. If she is not, she should die."

Melissa, a beautiful Puerto Rican junior with long, flowing red hair, is shocked. "Oh, my God. You're always hanging and killing and stoning. Where are you coming from? What about the husband?"

"The husband should be hung for killing the mailman. The wife should be hung for having the affair."

All the girls scream, laugh, and shout at Zuzu. And the quintet of boys, who sit around him, begin to clap and cheer. Laura's head drops to the desk with a loud thud, her hands cover her eyes. Finally she turns and glares at Zuzu.

Zuzu smiles back at Laura and continues to speak out. "If a man commits adultery, he should be punished, but not punished like a woman."

"Why do you make the distinction?" the teacher asks.

"That's the way I was brought up."

"But that doesn't really tell me anything. Why do *you* make the distinction?"

"Basically, because I'm a man. I'm more faithful to men than to women."

The girls are boiling over with rage. Hirsch tries another approach. "Does that mean that because you, Zuzu, are a male, men should be treated differently than a woman?"

"Yeah. Women are equal, but men are a little more equal." Zuzu holds his ground.

"Do you agree that you are a man because the sperm that fertilized your mother's egg had a Y chromosome? If it had been an X chromosome, you would have been a girl."

"That's true."

Melissa takes over. "Then how would you feel if you were a girl and someone said this to you?"

"I would take it as normal."

Laura can no longer remain quiet. "What makes you think that women are inferior?"

"I never said they were inferior," Zuzu replies patiently. "I said they were unequal."

A barrage of "yes-you-dids, no-I-didn'ts, well-you-meant-its" flies around the room.

Laura says, "By acceding to the conclusion that women are unequal, you set it up that women are inferior. The woman gives up her life for having an affair and the man gets a small punishment."

"Not a small punishment. A large punishment. But a smaller one than women."

Laura shouts, "You're setting up a disparity right there."

"So?" says Zuzu, and the others are yelling. Melissa wants to know what the difference is between a man cheating on a wife and a woman cheating on her husband.

Zuzu replies, "There's more temptation for men than for women."

The girls are screaming, "Oh, my God," and the boys are still clapping. Hirsch just barely holds on. Everyone is yelling and shushing at the same time. Hirsch tries to ask a question, but is interrupted by Melissa. She angrily explains women's sex drives to the boys. "We have plenty of temptation. And we do it when we want to do it. And you guys are so stupid that you don't know about it."

With some difficulty Hirsch finally settles everyone down and asks Zuzu to explain his statement. Zuzu relates his interpretation of the Islamic approach to sex. "In every society a man is stronger sexually. There is more pressure on a man to be tempted by a girl than a girl to be tempted by a guy. I believe that. It is human nature. I'm not the only person who thinks this way. Millions of people think that way."

"And they're all men!" shout the girls.

Laura becomes very upset by Zuzu's remarks. "How dare a man say that he can punish me for a crime that he would not be punished for? That's just bullshit. That's when rape happens. That's when mental and physical abuse to women happens. And it is unacceptable. I don't care how you are brought up. If you are brought up as a woman in a Lebanese society, and can't show who you are, that's your business. If you feel that you want to cover yourself so as not to tempt a man, hey, do it. But it has to be the woman's choice, not some man telling her to put a black bag on her body. That's bogus."

She isn't finished. "I should be killed for having an adulterous affair when a man goes free for the same affair? I'm outraged! It's bullshit that a man has a super sex drive and can't control himself. You've never been inside my body, you've never been inside my mind, you have no right to say that. My sex drive is just as strong as yours.'' All the girls, along with a number of the boys, give Laura a standing ovation.

But Laura is still not through. "And all you people clapping and laughing"—the boys immediately drop their hands—"I hate that. That's like patting someone on the back for date rape. AAAAAAAGH!" For the first time since the class began, the room is quiet. Both Zuzu and Laura remain resolved in their convictions. Zuzu is calm. Laura is aggravated.

Finally, Lenin, who did not clap with the other guys, raises his hand to speak. He wonders what would happen if Zuzu's mother or his sister were in this situation. "I don't think you'd want them to be stoned to death."

Zuzu looks calmly at Lenin. "My mother wouldn't cheat on my father because she knows the punishment."

"So that's why she wouldn't cheat?" asks Hirsch.

"My father told me that if I had a sister, and she got pregnant, he'd kill her. That is proper in Islamic society."

Hirsch asks another question. "You don't have to answer this question if you don't want to. I'm wondering if your father would cheat on your mother?"

"No. He was brought up not to. He was brought up not to steal."

The teacher tries to move away from the major players. "I heard a lot of applause when Zuzu talked about men being more tempted than women. I would like to hear from some of the other guys now."

Although Gabe says that he doesn't believe in a double standard, he does not think that girls should be allowed to do everything that guys can do. For example, he says that televised sports should be reserved for men. "I think the game would go slower. I've seen girls try to play football—"

"Try? Try?" Gina rises from her seat, her hands on her hips. Gina is on the girls' volleyball team, a winning team.

Gabe is not intimidated by her. "I hear them argue for equal rights. Then, when they don't want to do something, the men have to do it. They don't argue for things that they don't want to do."

Hirsch tries to switch to an analogy close to Gabe's heart. "Before Jackie Robinson was in baseball, people said very much the same thing about blacks. How do you feel about that?"

Gabe, who is black, replies, "I don't feel good about it but I understand it.

I can understand that a prejudiced person thinks that way. It is the same way I feel about gay people. I'm prejudiced about gays. I know I am. I don't want gay people to have any rights whatsoever. I can't stand even being in the same room with them. I think they should be put away somewhere." A hush falls over the room. Gabe persists. "I know what you are going to say: that is the position that some people take about black people. But where race is concerned they are wrong, and where gays are concerned, I am right."

The class moves into the subject of homophobia. By now the mailman, the husband, wife, and lover in the Brazilian short story are long gone. On this day Hirsch chooses to go along with the new twist because he is concerned about Gabe's attitude. He asks Gabe, "Why do you think blacks should have rights and gays should not have rights?"

"Because we were born black. I don't think gay people were born gay."

Laura is the only person to correct him. "Some scientists suggest that they are born gay."

Chang, a Chinese boy who had not said a single word throughout the semester, raises his hand. "About women in sports, I don't agree with Gabe's opinions at all. And about gay people, some people think it is a guy caught in a woman's memory." The class continues in this vein for quite some time. There is no yelling, screaming, or clapping. However, harsh homophobic exclamations ring out. Hirsch, Laura, and Zuzu are among the few who take up for the gays.

Gabe is becoming extremely upset. Even though it was he who brought the subject up in the first place, he says, "I don't want to keep talking about the topic. It bothers me."

Finally the bell rings.

CHAPTER 13

"I'm a Terrible Hispanic Person"

THE following morning, before school begins, a student from the class drops by Mr. Hirsch's room. He hands the teacher a piece of paper. Hirsch skims the page for subject matter. The student says, "I want you to read this to the class. Don't say my name."

Hirsch nods and says, "At the bottom you say, 'A student from this class.' Do you want me to read that?"

"Yes."

Later, during the reading of the paper, the teacher is careful not to say "he" when he refers to the person. The essay is a reaction to the homophobic remarks made the day before. The writer is a closeted gay student.

With the exception of Gabe, the class reacts to the poignant essay with care and compassion. Another lively classroom discussion takes place, with Zuzu, Laura, Maggie, and Denise doing much of the talking. The author just sits there, right next to the very person who brought up the subject in the first place: Gabe.

Lenin

LET'S start this way: I'm gay. I need to say that. In class, when we were talking about gay people, I didn't get a chance to say anything. I knew that if I said anything, I would have brought myself out of the closet, and I'm not ready to do that. I'm not ready to handle the bad attitudes or the bad comments. I've come out to most of my close friends, but I haven't come out to everyone.

I really felt bad when Gabe said what he did. I felt like he was throwing stones at me. Since I have to deal with these problems at home, I don't want to deal with them at school.

Yesterday, after school, I went home and started thinking about how I could get my part in. I couldn't sleep. I did not sleep at all yesterday. Early in the morning I started writing an essay. I asked Mr. Hirsch to read it to the class because I just had to have a part in that discussion. I really felt so bad.

When Mr. Hirsch started to read my essay, I was afraid that everyone would be looking around the room to see who the gay person was. I changed the way I was sitting. I spread my legs apart and took on a macho pose because I didn't want anyone to think it was me.

One girl asked who wrote the paper. I wanted to stand up and say it was me, but I was too afraid. I'm really scared that people will lose respect for me. I can't be in a room where people take me for a joke. I don't want people to see me and lift their wrists and blow kisses at me. I just kept quiet. I felt bad because I didn't say anything. I have a responsibility to tell people that being gay is not bad.

I wanted to clarify why gay people parade their gayness. Gay people have been suppressed for too long to simply say, "I'm gay," and that's it. When we come out, we really want to make it known. We wear buttons, we have parades, we want to tell everyone. I have some friends who do not know about me. Right in front of me they say, "He's a faggot." Or, "I can't stand faggots." Or they say, "Lenin, let's go out and beat up some faggots." I really have a horrible time.

If I could change just one person's mind, that would be wonderful.

Here's how I keep in the closet. For the first two months of a new semester, I never talk in class because my voice is very feminine. It has little wisps at the end. I was thinking about going to a speech teacher, but if I do, I will be hiding something that is a part of me.

I don't dress the way I want to dress. I don't want to come to school in drag or anything, but when I go shopping, I tend to choose unisex clothes that look more like women's clothes.

Lenin

I try to walk differently. I usually stand up straight with my head held high. My friend Robert said that it is really gay of me to walk straight and look up. He said that I look like a faggot when I do that. So now I look down, droop, round my back, and try to look like a bum. I don't make many friends because I don't want to tell too many people. I keep a low profile.

I'm Dominican. Most Hispanic men are supposed to be macho, and I don't fit into that at all. I'm a terrible Hispanic person.

I recently found out that everyone in my family knows about me. I only told my mother, but I guess she told everyone else. Mothers do that. I never tell my father anything, but I know that he knows. And I think he knows that I know that he knows.

After I told my mother that I was gay, I never heard her say a bad thing about gays. Before, she did. When there was something on TV about gay bashing, my mother would say, "Oh, they deserve it." And I would feel terrible.

Here's how I came out to my mother. My friend Robert had been encouraging me to tell my mother that I was gay. I wanted to wait and tell her after I move out of the house and go to college. One day Robert was visiting me. After he left, my mother asked me why I was hanging out with "that faggot." I said, "He is not a faggot."

She said, "That's what people are saying. You should really watch out who your friends are."

She was watching a soap opera. I said, "You should look out for me, not what other people are saying."

"Why? Is there something wrong?"

"Well, I'm gay." I was very nervous. I was sweating. My heart was beating really fast. My palms were really sweaty. I was glued to the chair, but I knew that I had to get up and turn off the TV. My mother was in shock. She hadn't smoked for two months, but she grabbed a pack of cigarettes and started smoking. "Lenin, I didn't hear that."

"Oh, yes you did, you heard it, I'm gay."

She looked at me. "You can't be gay. You haven't done anything. You're confused."

"Mother, I'm not confused. I've known this for a long time."

"How do you know? Have you ever had sex?" I told her that I had had sex. She kept questioning me about it. I didn't want to tell her much because it was with someone she knew. Then she said, "Well, try to keep away from them and you'll become less gay."

"How can you become less gay? When you are gay, you're gay." She wanted to hit me but she didn't. She controlled herself even though we were screaming at each other. In the end we hugged each other. She told me not to worry, that everything was going to be okay.

I've always know that I was gay. I've never really denied that to myself. Never in my entire life. It is something that I have always been proud of. I meet many people who lead terrible lives because they have to lie so much. They lie to their family and they lie to their friends.

Our family lived in the Dominican Republic until '85. I was eight when we moved to New York. Here I saw more positive role models. All the gay people who I had met in the Dominican Republic were either hairdressers or had something to do with fashion. When I came here the first man I met, who was not flamboyant, was with a friend of mine. He was gay but he didn't act like a gay person. He changed my whole view of it. After that I felt freer.

I have a younger brother and sister who are both straight. My brother and I get along. My sister I can't stand. She's a brat. I sometimes hate her because she's a girl. She's the smallest one in the family, so she takes a lot of attention from me. I don't really get along with my mother. I hardly know my father.

When my mother lets me go out, I go to nightclubs. I go dancing with my friends. I go to the movies. If I'm with my gay friends, we go to a gay club. I watch a lot of gay films. Not gay sex films, just gay films. Everything that I do revolves around my gayness. I have to be part of my community.

My mother says, "If you stop being with those people, you will stop having those thoughts."

What I really, really want is a true love. Right now I'm going through a cruising period. I don't do dangerous things because I'm afraid of AIDS. I won't have actual intercourse with anyone. I've had sex, but only with kids who are my age. That's a bit of a problem because I have a passion for older men. Thirty. Thirty-one. Anyone above twenty-five. I like my men to know about life and to know about being gay.

This is an awful thing to say, but I have problems with lesbians. I dislike them. I think it's such a waste. I shouldn't say a waste. Waste is not the right word. I don't want to offend anyone. When I see two pretty girls together, I wonder why they don't like guys. I contradict myself.

I can see a guy giving comfort to another guy. But with two girls . . . Two guys can offer a lot to each other, protection for one thing. Guys can be more affectionate than girls. I've only been around straight girls. The first lesbian who I ever met was Rachel. She is changing my opinion. I know that what I'm saying is bad, and if Rachel hears it, she will be disappointed in me. When I see a girl who looks butch, it annoys me. When I see a boy who is femme, I like it.

I always wanted to be a girl. Then, when I see girls wanting to be guys, I don't understand why. I like being a guy, and I like being gay, but if I had a choice, I'd rather be a girl. Girls get more attention. Girls can be sexy and flirty.

Advice From the Closet

IF you're going to be in the closet, at least come out to your very close friends. It makes it a lot easier. And if you *can,* not that you *should,* come out to your parents.

I have a wonderful coming-out plan. I'm a sophomore. Starting next year I'm going to change drastically. I'm not going to be so shy. I'm going to wear things that I really like to wear. I'll take off part of my mask. When my senior year comes along, I'm going to come out to anyone who asks. Actually, I will be out once the other kids read this book. I'm going to take a guy to the prom. At first I thought about going in drag, but I can't do that. I want to make a statement that being gay is normal. I hope I have someone to do it with.

CHAPTER 14

Portraits

FOUR students from Mr. Hirsch's English class, Laura, Zuzu, Oscar, and Gina, share personal views that include their religious beliefs: Judaism, Muslim, Jehovah's Witness, Catholicism, and a touch of Voodoo.

Laura

LET me give you a little background first. There are three branches of Judaism: Reform, Conservative, and Orthodox. Even though my parents are not Orthodox, the most traditional branch of Judaism, they sent me to an Orthodox school, called a yeshiva, because they wanted me to have a good education. I did get a good education, a very good education, but I was not happy.

A yeshiva is stricter than anything you can ever imagine. Boys and girls are not allowed to touch at all. We have to wear uniforms. We pray three times a day. Half the day is devoted to Hebrew studies, such as the Old Testament, and is taught in Hebrew. The other half is devoted to a regular, secular education, and is taught in English. I went to the yeshiva from kindergarten to eighth grade.

In kindergarten, I wasn't aware of the different stigmas placed on the non-Orthodox Jews by the Orthodox Jews. When my teacher told us to draw a picture of our favorite food, I drew a pork chop. Pork is considered non-kosher, that is, not conforming to the Jewish dietary laws. It is forbidden for an Orthodox Jew to eat pork. My family practices the most liberal form of Judaism, Reform. Reform Jews do not observe the dietary laws. When the teacher saw what I considered to be a beautiful rendition of a pork chop, he looked at me kind of funny. I didn't understand why. After that, for the next nine years, the kids teased me. I was called "pig" and "not a real Jew."

When I was called pig, I thought that there must be a weird side to me. After all, I was the only one out of 799 students who ate pork. I thought, "Maybe I should keep quiet. Maybe I shouldn't eat pork anymore."

From the first to third grade, I cried every day. I couldn't stand the teasing. Finally I figured out a way to deal with it. I learned to make fun of everything, make everyone laugh, and, most important, make them forget about making fun of me. My plan worked well and I made many friends.

But I couldn't meet my friends on Saturdays because Orthodox Jews don't drive on the Sabbath. They walk to synagogue. I couldn't invite anyone to my house for a meal because my classmates were forbidden to eat from any dishes that once served non-kosher food. I felt like an outcast.

Curiously, the one person who really respected me for who I was, in spite of my non-kosher ways, was the principal of the school. The principal is also a rabbi. (A rabbi is a spiritual leader of a Jewish congregation and is authorized to interpret Jewish law.) All the teachers in the school are rabbis. He taught our fifth-grade class my favorite subject, Gammara, which is the book of arguments. The principal and I would have intellectual arguments in the classroom. I enjoyed that so much. Then, because the principal respected my opinion, the students began to accept me for who I was and not for my jokes.

At the yeshiva, boys and girls attended classes together, but 99 percent of the attention was paid to the boys. Most of the learning in Judaism comes through arguing and coming to one's own interpretation of a text, within the boundaries set by the rabbis. Where learning is concerned, female students are not treated equally with male students. Women are not supposed to, or even allowed to, express themselves in class. I forced the rabbis to listen to me. I

Laura

insisted that I was entitled to as good an education as the boys. Whenever I gave my opinion, most of the rabbis put me down by their sighs and their body language. It made me very angry. Not being allowed to learn really got to me.

When I was fourteen I graduated from the yeshiva. I decided to forsake my Jewish education and go to public school. I was nervous about meeting the many types of people who go to public school. Would a person like me fit into such diverse groups as the punks, the hippies, or the club people who are into style and fashion? The fact that they came from different religions, or were of other races, wasn't a problem for me. I wanted to get away from everyone coming from one group.

During my freshman year at Humanities, I quickly realized that I fit in just fine. I felt like a kid in a candy store. "Oh, I can do that? . . . Oh, I can say that? . . . Oh, I can eat that?" Many people, students and teachers, had radical views. I met a number of feminists. And everybody seemed to talk about their feelings. It was great.

I went through a period of rebellion at home. I refused to observe any of the Jewish holidays. I even remained silent at my own family's loose observance of the Sabbath on Friday evenings. It felt good not to be restricted by the prayers and the laws. By this time, feminism replaced Judaism. However, for some reason I still found myself speaking with pride about the yeshiva and the lessons that I learned there.

I joined the drama club, stage crew, and a women's group. I was in student government and Humane Humanities. I took advantage of everything that the school had to offer. There is a core of activist kids here. I became part of that core.

During the second semester of my sophomore year, I was an exchange student in Budapest, Hungary. It wasn't until I found myself halfway around the world that I found pride in being Jewish.

One day, when I was feeling quite confident in my ability to speak Hungarian, I ventured into an unexplored section of the city. I knew that this section contained a Jewish synagogue and a rabbinical school (rabbinical schools teach rabbis). It was the largest synagogue in Eastern Europe. I thought it might be interesting to stop in and attend a service. I wanted to see if their cantor (a singing clergyman) was as good as my father, who is a cantor as well as an opera singer.

There is no way to describe this synagogue. It takes up an entire city block and is one of the most beautiful buildings I have ever seen. I immediately became filled with an uncontrollable curiosity to know everything about the Jewish community and the history of Hungarian Jews. My Hungarian was not as good as I thought it was, so I spoke to the caretaker in Hebrew. When the caretaker heard me speak Hebrew, I was treated like a long-lost relative. Actually, I may well have been his relative. My ancestors came from a small town 200 miles away in the northern part of Romania.

Once there were 600,000 Jews in Budapest, and now there are sixty. As I listened to the caretaker talk about the Nazi holocaust, I felt part of a family struggling to fight extinction. Here, in a country that was stripped of its Judaic culture, I reclaimed my Jewish heritage.

In one afternoon I not only gained 6,000 years of history, but I felt proud in calling myself a Jew. I finally let go of all the animosity that I had had at the yeshiva.

I can't work feminism into Judaism, but I can celebrate both. I am comfortable with both roles. I am a Jew who is very proud of her heritage and a feminist who is pretty staunch in her beliefs. I don't go to synagogue every week, but when I do go, it does hold something special for me. I want to go back to learning about my culture, traditions, and laws.

In my history class, or herstory class (I hate that word. It's so silly and people use that all the time), I'm proud when we study law. The logic of the law comes very easily to me because I learned how to argue in the yeshiva.

I love arguing with Zuzu. He sits behind me in class, so I can't see his expression when I say something. He seems to be listening. We have very different views. But so far we keep our arguments in the classroom and then say hi in the halls, like nothing happened. He doesn't seem to be anti-Jewish. That kind of stuff has calmed down here. I don't know why. Maybe there are just other issues.

I've come to the conclusion that I'm not Ms. Liberal and I'm definitely a racist. I think everybody has some racism in her. I'm learning to accept mine in order to let go of it. If I'm alone in the subway, and a black man walks on, I'm more afraid than if a white man walks on. I attach certain stereotypes to people just because of their color. I'm trying to get over that. Zuzu is helping me let go of the things that were pounded into my brain about Arabs.

Just last week I visited my yeshiva. It didn't bother me one bit when my old rabbi glanced disapprovingly at my pro-choice T-shirt. I am Jewish but I am a strong woman, too.

Zuzu

NUMBER one, I'm an American. I was born here. I go to American doctors. I'm taught by American teachers. America is big time. Number two, I'm an Arab. When I hear an Arab leader say something good, I feel proud. I say to myself, "I'm an Arab." Number three, I'm a Muslim. When I hear a Muslim leader say this, this, and that, I think to myself, "Yeah, I'm a Muslim." The emotional clashes between being an American and an Arab-American are strong. I don't want to disrespect people in my country by saying that I'm Lebanese. And I don't want to disrespect my heritage by saying that I'm not Lebanese. Sometimes my feelings about both cultures smash into one another.

My parents come from a very different culture. They do things differently from the parents of my American-born friends. They look different from the other kids' parents. When I was a little kid I went to the junior boys' New York Athletic camp. A lot of rich American kids go there. My parents were sitting on a bench eating their lunch. I heard the other boys whispering, "Look at Zuzu's parents. . . ." They said it in such a way like we were shit. I felt terrible. My father is a director at the New York Athletic Club, a very expensive club. If you compare the way my parents dress to the way rich people dress, the lawyers and doctors, my parents are lower than they are. Not as human beings, but socioeconomically.

My father is the greatest influence in my life. He used to be big time. He was "Mr. Lebanon 1954–56." My father is a nice guy. He's a hard worker. He looks out for his family. He likes to avoid problems. He hates to hurt people. Everybody loves him. I do, too. I wouldn't want any other father.

Before moving to New York, he lived in Liberia. He traveled around because there was no work in Lebanon. Plus he wanted to go out and explore. Once

he came to America, he decided to settle down here. But first he returned to Lebanon, met my mother, married her, and moved here. Though my father is Lebanese, he always tells me to be American.

My father gives me advice. He tells me to do good in school and to work hard. That's the biggest thing: working hard. Staying out of trouble. Be a good kid. Don't take drugs. Don't smoke. Don't hang out with the wrong crowd. Have good friends. Become a doctor.

The Lebanese are big on that. The main goal of Lebanese-immigrant parents is to work sixteen hours a day and put their kid through college. If a kid doesn't do well in school, he dishonors his family. If I come home with a bad report card, my father says, "You are just going to be another average person, breaking his back for a living. You have to learn to earn."

My mother doesn't teach me any beliefs. She feeds me. She worries about me. She tries to turn me into a mama's boy. That's what all Arab mothers do. They feed their kids all kinds of stuff. And they always hold them and hug them. It gets to be a bit much.

It is hard to be an American and speak English, and have an Arab mother. My mother doesn't have an education. She speaks broken English. She's over-weight. I wouldn't want my wife to be like that. My mother is a school-crossing guard. She works hard and then comes home and cooks and cleans.

We are a middle-class American family. In our home we celebrate Thanks-giving like any other American family. We have a big turkey and everything. We invite the relatives over. We thank Allah for a chance to come to America and be somebody. We're big on that. My mother serves my father. I grew up with that, so it is natural to me. In other American homes the woman cooks and the man makes the money. So what's the difference?

My parents have very different ideas about the way a teenager should behave. I'm sixteen and I still haven't dated a girl. That's bad. I should. Everyone else is doing it.

My parents say that before age twenty-one, Muslims are not allowed to go out at night. I go anyway. But if I come home at three o'clock in the morning, my parents want to know where I went.

I don't drink alcohol. Muslims aren't supposed to drink. I don't want to disrespect other Arabs by drinking alcohol. I don't want to drink anyway because I know the effects of it. Our family celebrates Ramadan. (Ramadan is the ninth month of the Muslim year, during which time Arabs fast from sunrise to sunset.) Every year I tried to fast but was never able to finish out the month. Last year my friend Omar and I fasted together. It was really hard. When we went to the lunchroom, all the other kids were eating. Some of them made fun of us. They would wave food at us and think it funny. For me it wasn't funny at all.

My father taught me that a girl cannot do the same things that a boy can do in the Islamic world. If a lady cheats on a man, she dies. I've changed. I changed my ideas about women because I realize that you can't live that way. I think women should be equal. If a lady cheats on a man, I feel pissed but I wouldn't want her dead. I believe in the death penalty but not for adultery. Sometimes I say things in class because I like to argue. That's a stupid part of my personality and I have to change that. I'm not so extreme that I believe that a woman should walk behind a man.

I don't want to brag, but I have such a good heart. When I see someone get beaten up, I feel so bad for them. That's why I have such strong anticrime feelings. I've seen people chased with knives. I've seen people pickpocketed.

I have to work in order to go to college. I work during the summers. My father said he will try to put me through, but it's a lot of money. I want to become a chiropractor. I like to help people.

Because my father is a director of the New York Athletic Club, I'm used to being around people who have a lot of money. Then I go back to my apartment on 46th Street, where the drug dealers and the prostitutes hang out. In a way, though, I don't mind seeing all that because I will be stronger in the long run. I know how to take care of myself on a rough street, how to deal with stress. If I ever become rich and powerful, I'll never forget mopping floors at the A & P. I still have the calluses.

When I worked at the A & P, the rich white people would come in from their offices with their big, snobby attitudes. They would walk on my just-mopped floors and not give a shit about it. They complained about every other price. And the stuff that they bought! My mother would never buy such stuff. I knew they were buying for their gourmet dinners and this and that. Filet mignon and salmon steaks. I felt like saying, "What do you need all that stuff for?" Rich people sure know how to waste money. Big-time wasteful.

At the A & P, I had to deal with homeless people like crazy. They smelled so bad and they always gave me a hard time. Every single one of them. That's why I hate homeless people. After that job, I wasn't for the homeless. They are healthy, they don't care about others.

Instinct tells me to be loyal to whatever I do. I was even loyal to the A & P. I had many opportunities to steal but I never did. I would never steal. I have some friends who do steal and I can't get them to stop. I think less of them when they do it. Almost every friend of mine hops the train. I'm the only one who pays. There are times when I hope an undercover cop will bust all of them. They deserve it, even though they are my friends.

People stereotype all Muslims as backward and as terrorists. I feel the need to straighten them out. The statement that all Muslims are terrorists is nonsense. Extremist groups do extremist things. And they should take the blame, not the people. The people are peace-loving. My friends and I hate terrorists. We hate violence.

The idea that we are backward is a biggie. To me, that's a bigger insult than saying we are terrorists. People say that we are not as smart as Europeans are. We are thickheaded. And yet, during Europe's dark ages, the Arabs and the Muslims led the world in learning, they developed a lot of things.

I have many Jewish friends. I have a Jewish friend who goes to Bronx Science. He knows that I'm an Arab. He knows that my parents are from Lebanon. I called him during the Gulf War and he said, "Zuzu, I'm so glad you called me." I felt really, really good about that. I would hate to have our religions tear us apart. My parents say, "In America, don't be stupid. Be friends with everybody." They have Jewish friends, too.

I know that I have a big mouth. I have a need for attention, a need for power. That's in everybody. I talk truth, though. The other kids are always jumping down my throat when I make comments and I respect that. I would feel stupid if nobody snaps back at me.

In the sixties the blacks had those big Afros because they wanted to show people that they were black. Now homosexuals wear "Silence = Death" T-shirts to show that they are gay. They show off. I want to show people that I'm Arab. I have a big mouth. I like to show people that I'm Arab. I don't think I'm perpetuating stereotypes when I say anti-Western things, because I'm intelligent about it.

I've heard Laura's feminist point of view millions of times. Sometimes I even agree with her. For example, we have to stop rapists. I want to get rid of rapists, muggers, murderers, and crooked businessmen.

If someone makes fun of New York, I get angry. New York is big time. I'm proud of New York but I see the need to change it. I want to put all the criminals in jail and cut off their hands—no, no, I'm joking.

Oscar

IN this school there are many different people with different beliefs. I thank God that everybody has their own opinions. If they didn't our world would be so boring. Although our church sets specific rules about dating and marriage, I do have friends from different religions. I can't go out with them socially, or have intimate relations with them, but I enjoy being with them at school.

I personally believe that if you follow the Bible, you will go on to salvation. Your attitude toward Christ is what matters most. If you don't believe in Christ, you have no hope. I think about what will happen to people like Laura, who doesn't believe in Christ. She could change. That's up to God.

I'm a Seventh Day Adventist. I go to church twice a week, Wednesday nights and all day Saturday. Adventists believe in the Ten Commandments. We worship on Saturday, not Sunday. Our music is different. Other churches have a lively beat to their music, but we keep our music simple. We don't dance. We see dancing as a form of devil worshiping. We don't go to clubs. We don't drink. We go out on dates, but we try to limit dating to people in the church.

In elementary and junior high school, I was teased about my religion because we don't watch TV or shop on Friday night or Saturday. Kids teased me about missing all the good TV shows. I didn't really care. It was my time to do other things. People think that because our church has strict rules, like no TV on Friday and so forth, that we don't have any fun. Just because we don't enjoy ourselves the same way that other teenagers do, that doesn't mean that we're not having fun. On Saturday night, after sundown, we gather together in the church. We play games and hang out.

I play the piano. I read the Bible and I talk to my mother. When kids make fun of me, I tell them that everyone is entitled to their own opinions. They don't buy what I say, but I really don't care.

The hardest thing about my faith is that it does stop me from getting girlfriends. There are beautiful girls in this school. I've had to reject two or three girls. I can't go out with them because they would pull me away from the church. I have seen many examples of people leaving the church because of some girl.

Here's one example: I had a friend who was a deacon. A deacon is like an usher who also takes care of the church. Even though he was my age, he was going out with a girl from outside the church. He fornicated—more than once. He told me all about it. He was actually proud of it. After a while he got caught. Somebody told on him. A friend told on him. Me. I told on him.

I didn't want to tell, but the pastor started asking me questions when he saw the girl coming to our church all the time. He noticed her attitude toward my friend. She followed him all around. When he asked me, I told him. I couldn't lie to him.

Afterwards, the priest talked to the couple, to be sure that what I said was true. My friend admitted to the priest that he had sex at various times at his parents' house and at his girlfriend's house. As penance, my friend's name was erased from the church. He had the option to come back, and later he did. In fact, his girlfriend became a member too. When you are erased, you have to start all over again. You even have to be rebaptized.

I was born here, but my parents are from the Dominican Republic. We speak Spanish at home. My father works at night as a doorman in a fancy apartment house. My mom's a sewing-machine operator. I'm the only child. They are very strict with me.

My parents stress good grades and I study hard. My mother has been churchgoing for as long as I can remember. Recently, my father has been going with us, too.

When I fill out an application for colleges I refuse to put down my race. I'm afraid if I put my race on the application sheet some college might be prejudiced about my being Latin American.

My father drinks and I don't see him much, especially since he works at

Oscar

night. My mom is alone all the time. It is hard for her to live this way, going to bed alone. I'm not going to do that to my wife. I want to spend more time with my family and I'm going to have more than one kid. Being an only child is boring. My life revolves around school, home, church. I never play sports with my father. We watch TV and eat together. I talk more with my mom. She understands me.

The kids are really integrated here. I don't see anyone staying with one special group, except maybe the Dominicans. They sit together in the lunchroom while everybody else sits all mixed together. I enjoy the way the Dominicans are together. They are alive. They are crazy. They throw empty milk cartons at each other. They insult each other for fun. They use vulgar language. I just listen and laugh. Even though I can't see them after school, they accept me because I'm Dominican. I could be the biggest jerk in the school, but so long as I'm Dominican, in their eyes I'm okay. I don't think they are prejudiced toward others. They just like to hang around with people who they were raised with.

Gina

I AM from Jacmel, Haiti. Sometimes people hesitate when they find out that I'm Haitian. They immediately think of voodoo. They regard voodoo as a kind of black magic. It's not black magic. It's a religion, just like any other. The followers have a strong belief in God. They think that if a true believer asks God a favor, he will get what he asked for. Isn't that like any other religion?

Not every Haitian practices voodoo. The Catholic Church is the biggest influence in Haiti. It's always fighting with the police about who controls the country. Everyone in my family is Catholic, except for my father's mom, who is Protestant, and my mom's mother, who does in fact practice voodoo.

When my father moved to New York, he didn't know that my mom was pregnant with me. He wanted to make more money to take care of his family. When I was two years old, my mother joined my father in New York and my

maternal grandmother raised my brothers and sister and me. We visited my parents every summer. My mother insisted that we be raised Catholic. She doesn't believe in voodoo, although I sometimes see religious ornaments in her room.

At my Catholic school they didn't know about my grandmother's voodoo because I wasn't allowed to discuss it. While we lived in my grandmother's house, there were special days that we were supposed to worship the gods. My grandmother gave us a bath with leaves. They were smelly and we had to rub them on our bodies. We weren't allowed to take a shower to get the smell off. We had to sleep with it.

One day a priest came to our house and told my grandmother that he had a dream that somebody was trying to take her children's souls away. My grandmother wanted to protect us. She closed the windows and doors and shut off all the lights. In the morning she gave us a shower with fish—dead fish. We smelled like crazy. The house smelled like crazy.

We were dressed in red and black. We tied our heads with red and black scarves. Everyone was praying. Oh, my God, I was so scared. After all, I was only eight.

For three days we had the fish on us. We stayed in the house, couldn't go anywhere, couldn't talk to our friends. On the third day the priest came and began boiling a razor blade in tea. He called every single one of us—my brothers, my sister, and my cousin—to line up in front of him. The oldest were first, the youngest last.

The priest took the razor and cut a special mark on our upper arm. My oldest brother went first and said that it hurt. Then the others started crying. I just walked straight up to the priest and gave him my arm. I didn't cry at all. I just watched him cut a cross on me. He tied my arm up with cloth. The next day we could go out and play. We couldn't discuss what happened with our friends. That was not allowed.

In 1985 we moved to America. At first I hated school because I was the only person in the class who spoke French and Creole, not English. Once I learned English I made lots of friends.

Last year people were saying that Haitians are not allowed to give blood because they all carry the AIDS virus. That upset me a lot. At first I thought, maybe I have the virus. I talked to my mom, who told me not to think about it because it was not true. I said, "It must be true because the food-and-drug people said that all Haitians have it. And they should know."

When I went to school, all my friends were talking about AIDS. I wondered what they were thinking about me. Did they think that I had AIDS? Did they feel dread that I'm their friend? Are they scared of me? If a friend told me that she was busy and couldn't see me, I would become paranoid. Was it because of AIDS? I wondered if my friends washed their hands after they held my hand. My friends never pushed me away from them, but I pushed them away from me. That was the only time in my life that I felt ashamed of being Haitian.

CHAPTER **15**

Special and Regular

Special-Education Classes

ALMOST got into a fight with a skin because one of my friends was going slow down the stairs. The skin said, 'Get them special-ed niggers out of the way.' And I said, 'You got something against special-ed niggers, man?'

"He said, 'No.' My homeboy was in back of me and he said, 'Yeah, he does. He said something about special-ed people.'

"Then we was in the Village playing pool and I saw him. I pointed a pool stick at him. He came up to me and said, 'Yo, man, I saw you pointing the stick at me, man.'

"I said, 'Yeah, I don't like people who talk about special ed. You're no different from us. You still get in trouble and so do we. You do stupid stuff and so do we. You're no different from us.'

"He said, 'I don't want to have no static.'

" 'Get the (pause for a breath) off my face, 'cause I saw you. And my homeboy was right there when you said it. If you don't want to get hit, leave.' So he left.

"He was a white dude, man. And I'm not prejudiced. I got friends of all races, you know what I'm saying? I ain't got nothin' 'bout nobody. But when they start acting like that . . .

"As far as I'm concerned, it's over and I will have nothing to do with it. If he does it again, I ain't going to have no choice but my hands."

—Ronnie

DON Dellamore stands in front of his special-education literature and ethics class. He is delighted that Ronnie, who is one of his students, dealt with a conflict using words, not fists. The class is discussing the book *To Kill a Mockingbird*. The teacher encourages the students to contrast their personal observations and experiences with incidents in the book.

All the students in Mr. Dellamore's class appear happy to be there. They appreciate the extra attention and relish their academic achievements. Nevertheless, special-ed students often feel stigmatized by the rest of the school. When the mainstream students, otherwise known as the regulars, learn that a person is in special ed, they often ask, "What kind of handicap do you have?"

Chris, a very large Hispanic young man who sits in the center of the back row, says, "They think we're retards. We can't write. We don't know what's going on. We get blamed for all the bad things that go on in the school."

Amanda

I'M half Chinese, half Puerto Rican. Some people tease me for being Chinese. Some people tease me for being Puerto Rican. Mostly the Puerto Ricans tease me. When I talk Spanish, they say that they don't understand it.

I get my bad temper from my Puerto Rican father. I get my wacky craziness from my Chinese aunt, 'cause she is totally out of it. Nobody knows it, but I'm very shy. I'm shy when it comes to boys. If I like a boy, I tell someone else to tell him that I like him.

I finally met David and he likes me because I'm me. When he saw me he said, "This is a girl who I could really care about." We've been going on strong ever since.

David is French, German, Irish, Scottish, and English. Some people think that nationalities and races shouldn't mix. When we walk down the street, people look at us like, "What's he doing with her?" I love his hazel eyes. He's in regular. It could be complicated 'cause I'm in special ed. Some people also think that special-ed kids aren't good enough to go out with the regulars. When the kids in regular see that I'm on the special-ed floor, they say to my boyfriend, "What are you doing with her?" I have some friends who are in regular who know me for what I am. And I have some friends who think that I have learning disabilities.

For a while I was in mainstream. The teachers thought I could make it in regular. But I couldn't. Most of the time I didn't understand the work. My mind was all mixed up. I always felt like I was surrounded by walls. I couldn't keep up. Now I'm back in special ed and I am doing very well. I get 90s here.

In my old school, people came up to me and asked, "Oh, you're in special ed?" I never lied. They asked if special ed was for retarded or handicapped people. I said, "No, it's for people who are gifted and talented." That's what I told them.

In this school it is different. People don't say things like that here. I guess that means they are mature.

It is true that some special-ed kids are rowdy. They are always getting into trouble. Some of them have an attitude. Those special-ed kids give the rest of us a bad name.

I want the world to know about us special-ed kids. We're calm. We're smart. We're civilized. We get good grades. We share all our problems.

Aracella

I NEVER ask questions because I get scared in class. When I'm asked a question, the first thing that comes to my head is that everyone will think, "Oh, God, this special-ed person always has something dumb to say."

You know what happened to me? There was a teacher at my Catholic school who left me back in kindergarten. Now I ask myself, "What could I flunk in kindergarten?" She wanted us to draw a tree. I drew a tree for her. She said, "That's not a tree." I said, "It has green leaves and it's brown." I'll never forget that.

Aracella, Mr. Dellamore, and Amanda

Then I went to public school. They put me in a special elementary school because the teachers said that I was too timid for regular. But my grades were so good that they moved me to a regular junior high school.

In junior high school the kids teased me until the day I graduated. They said that I was stupid. Even the teachers said I didn't know anything. They treated me like I was not human. People kept tearing me down. They would say, "Why don't you go to a retarded school?"

When I was in regular there was one girl who always bothered me. One time she got a 45 on a test and I got an 80. I said to her, "I should be in regular and you should be in special ed."

Then that same girl needed help in science. I said, "Now you know the difference between stupid and not stupid. I passed the test and you did not. I'll help you because you need to pass the science test." She never called me stupid again. We even became friends.

That incident changed my life. From then on I was so happy and cheerful. I stuck up for myself. I know I'm smart. It's just that I'm scared when I have to answer a question in front of a group of people. I'm sure that the other kids will laugh at me.

Because I don't raise my hand much in class, my teacher has to call on me. The other day when the teacher called on me I thought that I didn't know the answer. But I decided to give it a try anyway. I thought, "Oh, God, I'm going to be wrong." I answered the question.

"Aracella, that's correct."

"I'm correct?" I look it up in my book. OOOOOH! I am correct. Am I dreaming? It *is* correct. I had to check it five thousand times.

CHAPTER **16**

"A Rug of Your Own"

The Fifth-Floor Hall

MR. Hirsch races about the school lining up students and teachers to participate in Ethnic Heritage Day, an annual event that takes place on or near Bayard Rustin's birthday. When he spots Mohammad, a newly arrived Palestinian, he invites him to take part in the Mideast workshop that Laura and Zuzu are running.

Mohammad is skeptical because he does not believe that his audience would be open to his views. Testing, he caustically asks Hirsch if it would be all right to display his *Intifada* (the Palestinian uprising in the West Bank) head scarf during the workshop. Mohammad is amazed when Hirsch says, "Cool."

Mohammad

WHEN I first came to this school, the students would shout, "Hey, you terrorist. You-I-don't-know-what. Are you going to bomb the school?" I got that a lot. I took it as a joke.

They didn't like it when I did not react to them. They called me names. I had many arguments with students about what's going on in my country and about the Persian Gulf War. I have a different point of view.

When the kids call me Saddam Hussein, I tell them, "You take it as an insult, but to me, this makes me happy. So keep doing that." It drives them crazy. Insults don't bother me as long as they don't become physical. The students never get physical, but you know, things lead to things.

On my first day in this school, we had a sub teacher for English. She asked everybody where we came from. When I told her that I was a Palestinian, she was interested to know more about Palestine and what was going on. I knew that the girl sitting next to me was Jewish when I first looked at her. I expected some kind of argument. I was right. This girl denied everything I said. I asked her if she had ever been over there. She had not. I told her I experienced a lot of stuff and I can show her on my body all that I went through. She said that Israel is a very civilized country and they would not do that. But they did. And they are doing it. You can't deny it.

The second day in class, I tried to talk to this girl. She said, "I'm reading a book right now. I can't talk." She avoided me all the time. I don't like making enemies. I like to make friends. I gave it another shot the third day. And then, little by little, she started talking to me when I wasn't talking to her. Now we talk to each other as friends.

The first week I spent in this school, I had a physical fight. This Puerto Rican guy didn't like me. Maybe because I was a foreigner. My English wasn't too good and he was making fun of me. I tried to be friendly.

On the fifth day of the school, I said hi to him. He said, "What the hell you saying hi to me? An asshole like you doesn't talk to a guy like me." He was trying to show off in front of the girls in the school.

I said, "If you don't want to talk to me, fine. I'm not desperate." I asked the teacher to change my seat because I didn't want to fight. She would not change my seat. The guy sat behind me and would push my chair and say, "After school I'm going to break your face."

I couldn't take it anymore. I was really angry but I didn't know anyone in this school. I didn't know how many people he knew and how many people he could bring around after school. They could hurt me. I wanted to get it over with, right there in the class.

I got up and went over to him and said, "Listen, if you got something to do, do it now. Show me what you got." He got up and raised his hand to hit me. Before his hand touched me, I knocked him down. Then he pulled a chair out

Mohammed

and hit me with it. I grabbed this chair and I hit him in the stomach and knocked him down again. Then I took control over him. I held him and kept holding him until the security guards came. I could have really hurt him, but I didn't want to do that. I don't want to make enemies. I want to make friends.

Everyone was yelling to let him go, so I did. He went for a chair again. Once again I held him. He was yelling, "Watch your back."

I said, "If I can get you once, I can get you again." We ended up in the dean's office and I got suspended. When I came back to school, he met me on the stairs with five guys. I went up to him and said, "Believe me, I'm not what you think I am. You've seen me alone here. And you've seen me trying to be peaceful. But once it gets to action, I'm very experienced in fighting, and I can hurt you a lot."

"We'll see after school."

After school I made a phone call and got five guys to meet me. When he knew I was backed up, he left me alone. A few days later he sent some guy to tell me that he wanted to make up and be friends. I shook hands with him. And we forgot about the past.

In one way I like it here, and in another way I don't like it here. First of all, I see myself losing a lot of my culture. I'm getting a little Americanized. Secondly, I'm away from my family—from my mother and my brother.

I lived in a very little village in the West Bank (currently in Israel), near the town called Ramallah. In my village there are 2,000 people. They all know each other. They are like one family.

My family lives in a big house with a lot of rooms. When I was little it was a little house, but we kept adding. My father moved to America to get a better job. He would send us money and we would build another room here and there. I lived with my mother, my little brother, and my older brother's wife. It was a very traditional life.

The first time I saw my father again was in 1984. We didn't get along with each other. He complained that I was raised by a woman. I told him, "That's not my fault. Where have you been when I was growing up?" He should have been there for me. Now it's too late to try to change me.

In my country there is a big difference between the city and the village. The people from the city are more Westernized. The women don't have to stay home and take care of the children. They go to work. In the villages it is more traditional. I don't agree with all the things we believe about the women. I think about this a lot.

In America the women are more free. That's not something I hate for a woman. But I don't like a lot of things they do. In this country I see a girl with different guys. I don't like this kind of girl. When I go out with a girl in this country, I make sure I am her first or second boyfriend. It is safer, sexually. Besides, a girl who hangs out with a lot of guys cannot be trusted. We never have this in my country. A woman is always loyal to her man. The men are loyal, too. I never have more than one girlfriend at a time.

In my country a woman has to respect her husband. She does whatever she wants as long as he says it's all right. She shares her ideas with her man before she does any action. And if the man says no, then it's no. Over here, a woman will do something without even asking her partner.

There are many religious people in my country. I was very religious. I used to spend all my time praying in the mosque. After a while, people were fighting and people were getting killed. I wondered, "What's behind this? Why is this going on?" I asked people who were older than me, educated people. They told me that this land was once a Palestinian homeland. The Israelis took over and controlled the people.

Let me explain it in this way. Let's say I own a house that we both lived in. Even though you have use of the same rugs that I have, wouldn't you want to have a rug of your own? Even though I give you everything you need, wouldn't you want to get things for yourself? Even if you could do whatever you want in this house, wouldn't you still want to be the owner? That's the same with us. We would like to have our Palestinian state, an independent one.

When people hear that I'm a Palestinian, they assume that I hate Jewish people. That's not true. I dislike the Israeli government, but I have nothing against the people. I have a lot of Jewish friends over there. I even went out with Israeli girls. My parents never knew about it because in our religion I'm not supposed to go out with girls, even Arab girls. Most of the girls that I went out with thought I was an Israeli or a Jew. The ones who knew still went out with me.

After a while my parents thought that I should move to America and live with my father. Economics played a big part in their decision. They thought I could find a good, decent job, where I could make a little money to help the family.

My father and I are not getting along together. First of all, when he was young, he was doing this same stuff that I am doing right now. He was going out with girls and things like that. Now he's against a man being with a girl who he is not married to. He is married to my mother and he stays away from other women. I'm not like that.

There are some things that he did when he was young that I would never do. He used to drink a lot. I've never had a drink in my life. Neither one of us ever took drugs.

My father thinks I'm not smart, that I don't want to work, that I don't want to do anything. I've always been working. I started working after school when I was twelve years old. He has no proof for what he's saying. But since he's the father, he's always right. Here, I have a good after-school job. I work downtown in a supermarket.

I believe in God. That's one of the reasons why I'm never scared. People can try whatever they want, but they can't change fate. If something is going to happen, it will be done by God, only by God.

During the Gulf War a black guy came into the supermarket where I work and asked, "Who's an Iraqi here?" He could tell that I was Arab by the way I look, so I said that I was an Iraqi. He said, "I feel like killing you."

I said, "Why don't you try that? It isn't that easy to kill me. You don't know nothing about me, you can't just kill me. Come on and do something."

He said, "Come outside." So I went outside with him. I believe that there is a time when you are going to die. Nobody can stop you from dying when that time comes. If this was my time to die, I'll die. If not, I have nothing to worry about. I put my hand inside my jacket pocket and told him to take his best shot. I had nothing under my jacket, but he thought that I had a weapon.

"Yo, hold it." He backed off.

I shouted, "Never mess with an Iraqi."

CHAPTER **17**

Teachers

Joan Jarvis

AS I look back at my career, I've always been very, very happy to say I'm a teacher. When people ask me what I do, I don't say that I'm an administrator or that I'm a principal. If they explore a little more, I'll tell them, but my first answer is, "I teach."

When I was nine years old, my family moved from New York City to Suffolk County, in Long Island. In those days it was very rural. There were potato fields, deer, and rabbits. I went to elementary school in Port Jefferson, a town that was considered a white community. In our school there were twenty black kids out of eight hundred youngsters. I didn't feel any different from the white students. My parents never made us feel that we were different.

I was always a very capable student, always competitive, always friendly. I think I am a friendly person. In elementary school and up through the eighth grade, I got nineties in everything. If students had very high grades, they went to high school a half year early. Once there, we could work toward an academic, a commercial, or a general diploma.

When I went into the high school, although I was considered one of the academic brains, the programming department put me into the commercial track, studying to be a secretary. My mother looked at my program and said, "No, that's not what Daddy and I want for you. I'll go to the school tomorrow." I realize now that what my mother was saying was, "My child is going to college, therefore she must have an academic diploma, not a commercial

diploma." If I was smart enough to go to high school a half term early, why was I was not smart enough to be in the academic track? I gather that I was placed where I was because I was black. That's the only thing I can attribute it to.

My parents were very careful to see that their children got what we deserved. They watched over us. My sister, my brother, and I were all academically oriented.

There were two hundred teachers on staff at the John Adams High School in New York when I was hired as a French teacher. I was the first black teacher. At my first open-school night there were so many parents visiting my classroom just because they were curious to see who I was. There was, however, one parent who came because he was very angry that I failed his youngster on his first report card. The student marched in with him. He had a look on his face that clearly told me, "Now-my-father's-going-to-get-you." I said to the father, "I'm sorry that your son failed, but let me share with you what he's done." I had kept all the student's homework and weekly test papers. As I showed the father the boy's work, the kid's face was falling farther and farther.

The father, who came in ready to kill this black woman, looked at his son and asked, "Is this record correct?"

The boy looked at me and I looked at him. Then he looked at his father and said, "Yes."

The father said, "Then how did you expect to pass?" He apologized. "Miss Woodbern (I wasn't married at that time), I came here ready to have you removed because I thought you were prejudiced against my child. I see that it was my child who was prejudiced against you. You will never have another problem with him." The kid didn't turn out to be a superstar, but I certainly never had a bit of trouble with him.

Along the way, friends and colleagues suggested that I should be in a position where I could affect more people. I became a department supervisor of the foreign language department, where I taught French, Spanish, and English as a second language. At that point someone said, "Think about how many more people you could affect if you were a principal. Besides, you need to make more money." So I moved up.

The truth of the matter is that I became an administrator because I was

Mrs. Jarvis and her students

black and female in a system that was obliged to acknowledge an overabundance of white males. I've never been really ambitious on my own behalf. Somebody has always put me in a position where I felt I could not say no.

At this stage, as a principal, I don't feel much prejudice because I'm a black and I'm a woman. I have a sense of who I am and I know that this is my chair. When other people don't know that, I let them know.

I've been at Humanities for four years. People tell me there is a different atmosphere at the school. I think it's probably my leadership style that makes people think there are changes. We still have the same good quality of teaching. We still have a lovely group of youngsters, but I think that I have brought more openness to the process. I'm an advocate for the children. They recognize that. They know that I am available to them.

The quality of our lives will never improve until we as people learn to live with one another. The negative stereotypes, the bad feeling that we have as one race to another, or one culture to another, really don't have much substance.

As educators there are things that we can consciously do to foster multicultural living. I encourage the teams and the clubs to make youngsters of various ethnic groups work together. Our chorus tends to be predominately black and the drama club white. I look at the chorus or the drama club when they are preparing for a performance to make sure that it is ethnically balanced. At the auditions, when decisions are being made about who is going to be the soloist or going to be the star, I have often said, "You must get more white students into the chorus." Or, "You must get more minority kids into the play." The youngsters who work together in a club, or a play, or on a team, begin to see that there's really no difference amongst them. That's very important to me.

It's only through the children that we will begin to improve our lives and to foster brotherhood. Youngsters are not so set in their ways that they can't be made to see that all people are basically the same. However, I don't think there's that much help for adults who have been raised in a certain way. I'm not sure that they can change.

I've also tried to make my school a kinder, gentler place. I really feel that all my children, whether they are from affluent families, poor families, or hotel children, are at risk. Kids today experience very little tradition. There is very little family cohesiveness and a great deal of fragmentation. The main thing that I can offer them is to make this school an island of stability.

One of the things that we do is to set a tone that prejudice is simply not acceptable here. I try to get the kids to know each other better. Often the students socialize with their own ethnic groups. In the cafeteria, for example, the Asians always sit together in one section while the African-Americans sit in another section. Sometimes I go up to the cafeteria and mix the students up. I tell them, "Let's all sit at different tables today. Let's visit with each other. That's the aim."

We really are the same no matter what cultural background we come from. Parents want their children to have better lives. They want them to be honest. They want them to have integrity. They want them to be able to get along in life. So we focus on those things.

My professional expectation is that when I say something to children, they are going to listen. In my auditorium programs I stand up there and say, "May I have your attention . . ." And it gets quiet. My expectation is that youngsters will listen because I'm the teacher. And they rise to the occasion. They are lovely children.

Russel Hirsch

I LOVE kids. And I love to help high school kids get turned on by ideas. There is so much they need to know. They can't always talk to their parents about everything. I like the fact that they can come to me and talk to me.

Some people may see me as a bleeding heart liberal just looking for a cause. I can't worry about what these people think. I have a great deal of empathy with the disenfranchised and the downtrodden. I find myself empathizing with the oppressed. It's a part of me that has always been that way. I'm a big supporter of the women's and the gay rights movements.

I grew up in an affluent, politically conscious family in Long Island. It is conceivable that I feel guilty about being born white, born male, and born into a family with money. I find it embarrassing to say that I grew up in Great Neck, because it is such a wealthy community. I tell people I am from Long Island.

In my town, busing was rejected by the school board and the PTA. I was very much in favor of blacks coming to my school. I'm not sure why. I just thought it was the right thing to do.

As a little kid, I was attracted to black role models. When I was into sports, Willie Mays was my hero. Once I got into music, Jimi Hendrix became my hero. Then, after I moved out of the rock scene, I became interested in black jazz. There were some technically fine white musicians, but they never reached my soul. White jazz was a little too sterile, too academic for me.

When I was growing up, there was a lot of love in our house, but there was a lot of resentment as well. My parents were very IQ conscious. My father, who is a doctor, preached success to my brother, my sister, and me. He would drive us to elementary school and say, "Be brilliant." Not, "Have a good day." Not, "Have fun." Be brilliant. As cute as he meant to be, it killed me.

My brother was a terrific athlete at our high school. He did very well academically. I had a good relationship with my brother, but I was jealous of him. He was so successful. And my father was so successful. I was a problem child, a rock-and-roller.

In the late sixties I had a number of experiences that made me want to fight racism. As a teenager, I went to a summer camp in Montana that was sponsored by the Ethical Culture Society. The camp was made up of a diverse population: poor people from Harlem, Native Americans, Hispanics. It was 1969, and people seemed to be trying to get it together.

When I was fourteen I went to a Black Panther meeting in New York City. I was recruited by a boy handing out pamphlets. I wanted to be a part of it, to hear their concerns. I didn't want doors closed on me because I was white. It must have been strange to see a white teenage kid walk into a Panther meeting. The people stared but they treated me well. It became important for me to be accepted by blacks.

I became a devout hippie. A longhair. I was into the electric guitar and sociopolitical interests. Around this time my brother was dating a black woman who is now my sister-in-law. My parents were cool about that, but not perfectly cool. They thought it would be strange to have black grandchildren. I thought that was a lame excuse. Now my parents couldn't love their grandchildren more. My brother and I like to joke that we brought our folks up well.

After high school I attended the Berkelee College of Music for a little less

Mr. Hirsch

than a year. A quarter of all the musicians there were guitarists. To be a jazz guitarist you either have to be the best or you end up doing jingles that are played in supermarkets. I thought I wasn't good enough to make it among the best guitarists. Also, there were very few women at the college. My love life was not good.

I reached the point where I wanted more from life than just music. I returned home to major in English at NYU and met my future wife. We've been together for thirteen years, married for seven. My wife, Daria, is pregnant and we will have our first child in June. I'm very excited about that.

Students who have been transferred out of the other music class, taught by Mr. Steward, say to me, "You know, it's funny, you got the white teacher on the second floor teaching black music and the black teacher on the fourth floor teaching white music." It *is* peculiar. People can read anything they want into this. They can read into it that I wish that I was black. But I don't think you can get anywhere with too much psychoanalysis of this. It's simply what I love.

Because I'm fascinated by the way that cultures musically influence one another, this school is tailor-made for me. I'm given a lot of leeway to be creative in areas that are very important to me. Mrs. Jarvis gave me the opportunity to develop a new curriculum in my music-appreciation course that focuses on African-American music. That's what I know best and that's what I'm most interested in. Although I love teaching this course, it does have its liabilities. Some white and Asian students are alienated by my approach. I hate to stereotype people, but there are times when I put a record on and the Asian kids take out their homework and begin writing. I resent that. When I tell them to put away their books, they do.

On Black Solidarity Day I was playing music by Miles Davis. A young white man walked into the room and muttered under his breath, "Do we have to listen to this nigger shit?" I really wanted to wring the kid's neck, but let it pass because I wanted to get the class going. I decided to wait and confront him later. A young lady in my room also heard it. Like me, she didn't say anything about it. When the class ended, she said to the boy, "Excuse me, I wonder if you could come up to the front of the room?"

He came up to the front. She said, "Mr. Hirsch, could you just be a witness to what I have to say?" She turned, looked the young man square in the eyes, and said, "I just want to tell you that what you said was extremely offensive. It offends me personally because I'm part black, but even if I wasn't, I think it was an extremely offensive remark."

In a non-confrontational tone, she defended me for playing that kind of music, especially since it was Black Solidarity Day. She was not condescending. She did not yell at him. She also said, "I'm telling you this not just for my benefit or the benefit of the class. I'm telling you this for your own sake. There may be a time when you make a stupid comment like that one and you get the shit kicked out of you. I think you should start thinking about your behavior."

Barbara Williams

I'M a native New Yorker, born in Queens. I am a product of the New York Public School System. As a child I sensed a lot of negative things, but I didn't know where they were coming from. I was one of two black kids in my school. I felt isolated from the white kids, but I never could put my finger on why. It wasn't until I started studying my own history and culture that I learned about the nature and history of racism. I saw how deeply racism is a part of American life. A lot of this stuff has become an integral part of our society, and that worries me.

I grew up in an integrated working-class community. My family lived in a public-housing project designed for working-class people. We all lived together and worked together without incident. During the civil-rights protests, I wish I could say that I was conscious of the problems, but I wasn't. I never went on the marches.

I had an Irish friend and we were very close, but I wondered why she would never come into my house. I was always in her house. I found out that her family told her never to go to my house.

I went to an all-girls' high school. There were only a few black girls. I would go to dances with the local boys' school and not dance. White boys weren't interested in me. I wasn't interested in white boys, either. During the dating years, my white friends and I began separating from each other.

When I first graduated from high school, I decided that I wanted to be an airline stewardess. I went to an employment agency in Times Square. The interviewer looked at me as if I were crazy. It wasn't until much later that I realized why. There were no black stewardesses. It never occurred to me that you had to be a certain color.

By the time I was in college, the whites started moving out of our neighborhood and non-working families moved in. At Queens Borough Community College there were times when I felt alienated. I was one of only two blacks, both female. There weren't any males of my racial background around.

Later, I went to Manhattan Community College for a degree in computer programming. My accounting professor, who was male, white, and Jewish, said that he understood that black people had difficulty with mathematics, that it was hard for us. Even though we usually didn't do well, he was going to help us anyway.

While I was at Manhattan Community College I started studying African-American and African history. Many of the things that had happened to me, that I didn't understand, began to make sense.

About that time I married my first husband. We looked for an apartment in a two-family home in Queens. The homeowner said, "I know you will want to have a lot of parties and this is a quiet neighborhood. This isn't the right place for you." I'll never forget that, either.

After our son was born, I became determined that he wouldn't have to put up with the little insults that I put up with. I became very vocal, making up for lost time. Now I go to demonstrations and I'm involved in a church that is politically active. I made sure his teachers knew that he had parents, a mother and a father, who would be there at the drop of the hat if anything unacceptable was going on. It is very important for a parent to be a strong presence in the schools.

My son is now seventeen years old. He is a freshman at the University of Rochester. I'm sighing with relief that he is a high school graduate. I'm sighing with relief that he can read and write and speak English. I'm sighing with relief that he's not dead. My son is a target for so many people's guns. An African-American mother worries about that.

Part of the reason why I decided to change careers and become an educator was because of the influence a good teacher has on a great number of people.

Ms. Williams

What a teacher says remains with students for the rest of their lives. I certainly remember the teachers who influenced me.

I had a good education. I have a love of literature and a love of history because of the schools that I went to. But I also would have benefited from seeing more black role models. I had only one black teacher in my whole student career.

When I teach American history, I try to interject things about Native Americans, things about Asian-Americans, things about African-Americans. I want to reach many people, not only those people who are of African descent.

I get respect from a lot of kids. I think the Asian kids and the white kids respect me, they care about me. And I care about them. I think they see that I'm fair and not trying to pull the wool over their eyes.

In general, African-Americans do not sit down with their kids and talk about their people and their history. My parents didn't. As a result many black kids have no idea who they are.

Black males are not motivated. By the time they reach junior high they are so disillusioned. They don't put in anywhere near the effort necessary to become minimally successful. They're *not* stupid. They are intelligent. But they do everything they can to make sure they fail. They don't come to class. They don't do their assignments. Whatever you ask them to do, they do the exact opposite or nothing at all. Some can be reached, but it takes a lot of work. It means reaching out and pulling them through.

Three black boys were in my office a few minutes ago. Earlier, I found them fooling around in the halls, laughing and calling one another nigger. I brought them in to talk about why the word nigger is unacceptable. "Nigger" was used by whites during slavery times to define black people as less than human, not worthy of any kind of respect. In this society a black person doesn't get much respect anyway. I don't want to see the kids insult themselves when they refer to each other in such a way. I told them, "If you must insult somebody, call him a fool, call him something else. But not that!" The kids simply don't have the background. They heard me. They won't use it around me, and maybe one of the three really understood what I was saying.

Most people don't know how destructive slavery was. They see the people who came from Africa as ones who have no goals, no plans, and no stake in this culture. Even though it ended quite some time ago, this is the result of slavery. To make slavery work, everybody had to believe that blacks were less than human, were unworthy of equality, were incapable of being relied on in certain areas, and, no matter what, would never be equal to whites. After slavery ended, we didn't do enough to change that mind-set. The systems that were created to make slavery work are still with us. They are still damaging and destroying people.

At this school there will be about two or three racial incidents in a semester. A significant number of incidents occur among the Hispanics. The Hispanic kids who come from many different cultures are all mixed together. They now live in a country where being black is not what one wants to be. The Hispanics believe that they have the option of not being black.

Recently, an Hispanic girl who has light skin attacked another Hispanic girl who has dark skin. The light-skinned girl had been taught at home that if you have light skin you are better, you're white, and you must stay away from the dark ones.

The blacks and the Asians have quite an interesting conflict. Here we have two groups of people, alienated from society, but trying to move within the society. They are performing in this alien community according to their own cultural rules. And their rules are very different from one another. The Asian kids get a lot of negative indoctrination about blacks from the parents. I'm saddened by that, but I am not surprised.

African-Americans and Hispanics feel threatened by the Asians. They sense that the Asians are more accepted by society and they feel left out—again. They think that the Asians are good students who don't want to make trouble, therefore they are easily intimidated. The conflict arises when the Asians get tired of being picked on.

I don't think we have a clear understanding of our cultural differences. We're not finding enough ways to bridge them. There are a few people in this school who are working hard to do that. But there are so many other things going on that it is very hard to give the time, the space, and the money to work things out. Something is being done; much more can be done.

Public-Speaking Class

MARK Thompson is one of the most popular teachers at Humanities High. He's smart, creative, open-minded, not to mention handsome—extremely handsome. Mr. Thompson teaches English and public speaking. He heads the drama club and is in charge of the school plays. Everyone tries to get into at least one of his classes.

In Mr. Thompson's public-speaking class, the assignment was to write and give a persuasive speech. When it was her turn, a Chinese student began a fervent speech against homosexuality. She explained that, as a Catholic, she follows the teachings of the Church. She described AIDS as if it were a scourge from God. Her general conclusion was that all homosexuals should die of the disease very quickly so that there would be no more homosexuals.

Thompson knew that he had to say something. There were too many inaccuracies, too many false conclusions, in her talk. He told her and the class that there have been homosexuals in every society throughout every age. In Greece it was accepted behavior that men loved one another. In many Native American cultures, homosexuals were revered. One reason why the Judeo-Christian tradition frowned upon homosexuality was because the leaders needed their numbers to grow.

Thompson didn't want his rebuttal to sound like a personal reproach. However, several of his friends had died from AIDS, and he felt very strongly about what had just been said.

While Thompson spoke to the class, he debated with himself whether or not to be more direct about the subject. "Here I was trying to teach these kids to speak up for themselves. All the while, I was keeping quiet. By speaking up, I could show them how to do it, too." After going round and round in his head while correcting the student's misinformation, he told himself, "Take the step, even if it is risky."

Finally Thompson took a deep breath and told the class that he was gay. Utter silence. Not a gasp. Not a murmur. Not a snicker. The teacher said that he had to give them that information in order for them to understand what he had to say about the subject.

Mr. Thompson

He asked his student if she had interviewed any homosexuals for her speech. She had not. He asked her if she knew any homosexuals personally. She did not. Then he asked her how she could give a speech on a group of people about whom she knew nothing. "I strongly implied that what she was preaching was hate."

The student was devastated. Thompson says, "I kept trying to reassure her that I knew she meant well. She was speaking from basic beliefs that had been instilled in her. But her beliefs included untruths, and I couldn't allow the class to walk away thinking that there was some validity to them. I had to challenge her. The entire period was then devoted to debunking the myths."

Religion almost always comes up in Thompson's students' speeches. He tells them that they are free to believe what they want, but when making a speech in his classroom they cannot proselytize or be offensive.

Mr. Thompson says, "I was very hesitant to come out and admit that I was gay because I knew that five minutes after the class changed, the rest of the school would know. Suddenly I didn't care. For so many years I kept my homosexuality quiet. I was afraid of being laughed at. I would hear people tell gay jokes. I smiled along with them, even though I found the jokes offensive. 'Keep your mouth shut! Don't let anyone know what you are, because you don't want to be discriminated against.' I'm at a point in my life where I just don't care. I refuse to be the object of discrimination. Once I came out, I felt powerful."

The day after the astonishing "out-of the-closet" revelation, many students came up to Thompson and put their arms around him. They were very protective. Here was an adult, a favorite adult at that, who was just as vulnerable as they were. "The kids were great. Some became more physical, the boys and the girls. They wanted to be touched. I think they realized that I wouldn't do anything to harm them. I was safe. They felt closer to me.

"The next day the student who made the speech came to apologize. I told her that she had nothing to apologize for. It took courage to take her position. There were no hard feelings. I admired her for following through on her speech. It may not be something that I agree with, but she has a right to her beliefs. But I also have an obligation to challenge the untruths."

Ever since that experience, the student has opened up to Thompson and, in fact, she's a lot warmer. She says how much she admires him because it took courage to come out.

A few weeks later Thompson casually mentioned his boyfriend, in passing, to his class. The kids noticeably twitched. He laughed at them. "You know I'm gay. I didn't say I'm a monk." On this day the class laughed with him.

Mark Thompson

I GREW up in a small town called Rockville, just outside Hartford, Connecticut. I have five brothers and sisters. I'm the second-oldest child, the oldest son. When my dad was my age, thirty-seven, he already had had six kids. He was constantly struggling to provide for us. As a result, he reacted against anything that threatened the stability of his job. During the sixties, when the civil-rights movement was in high gear and affirmative action was getting a lot of attention, my dad was struggling to provide for his children. You can rest assured that my father never picketed for affirmative action. My father is a redneck.

I was an altar boy. My summers were spent at religious camps where the priests would go out of their way to help kids have a great time. Kids from large blue-collar families didn't otherwise get much attention, and the priests made us feel special. I grew up wanting to be just like them. I went to a high school seminary and studied for the priesthood.

The seminary was a Catholic boys' boarding school. The first time I was ever exposed to homosexual activity was with an assistant dean, a brother. I was fifteen. I didn't know what homosexuals were and I was frightened to death when I found the brother was sitting on my bed, touching me in the dark. I reported him and he was dismissed.

In my Catholic school, I didn't learn much about sex. It was a different age and people were a lot more naive. I had been attracted to some of my male friends, but I didn't understand why. I would joke about "faggots" and "queers" and not know what I was joking about. I tried to look up the words that I heard in the dictionary, but those words weren't listed. I thought "queer" meant a really strange person. Even though I was attracted to men, I didn't think I was "that kind of person." The thought was repulsive to me.

In high school, I started masturbating and I was pretty guilt-ridden. It wasn't until I was in college that a priest told me that he did it, too, and that it was perfectly natural. That's when I felt there truly was a God.

I started dating girls in college, but I found myself still attracted to guys. I wasn't having sex with my girlfriends. It wasn't that I wasn't willing. The girls who I was going out with wouldn't let me have sex with them. But I never found myself getting particularly excited sexually. I was confused, so it was easier to abstain for the time being.

When I finally realized that I was gay, I thought that I was going to go straight to hell. My Catholic upbringing taught me that my thoughts were filthy and evil. I thought I was going crazy. I didn't know what was happening to me. I knew that I was supposed to be attracted to women. I wasn't attracted to women, and yet I was supposed to marry one and have children.

There was no one to talk to about it. I was able to tell the priests about masturbation because I was confessing to it as a sin. Never once did I confess to my feelings for boys. At confession I just called them "impure thoughts," and got away under general all-purpose coverage. When the priests probed, I made up some stock impure thoughts.

It wasn't until just before I graduated from college that I started experimenting with men. I was not comfortable having sex with them because of the religious thing. I was following a natural urge, but it was considered wrong. But I just wasn't attracted to women. It took me a long while to realize that there's nothing wrong with being yourself. What is wrong is taking advantage of somebody else, using somebody, anybody, just to have sex.

In 1985 my first lover left me. I thought we were monogamous. He had lied to me, and in light of the present health crisis with AIDS, I felt that I was left high and dry. Toward the end of our relationship, he was coming home very late at night. He had been going to the leather bars, leading a double life. I knew nothing about it.

Eventually he told me that our relationship was definitely over and he moved out. I was devastated. I went home and talked to my dad. When I told him that I was gay, the first thing he did was offer to pay for psychotherapy. I told him that I wasn't psychologically disturbed, I was gay. To this day he still can't understand how I can be attracted to a man. I'm his oldest son, and he has certain expectations that I can't meet. I won't give him grandsons and that is tough for him. At least my brothers have kids.

My present lover, Peter, and I have a really nice relationship. We have arguments now and then. Lately I've overextended myself. I snap a lot. But I find that our love is deepening. It's so different from the days when I first moved here, met somebody, had a one-night stand or saw someone a few times. I never felt comfortable with that.

Even though my siblings are supportive of us, Peter got a cold welcome from my dad when I brought him home with me. And my mother remained very aloof in order not to offend my dad. After that first experience, Peter doesn't want to go to my family's house. I go with him to his family. His dad doesn't totally understand us, either, but he loves Peter and wants him to be happy. He accepts me.

My mother is a very loving woman. For Christmas she sent Peter a Christmas stocking that she knitted with his name on it. And she also sent him a lovely thank-you note for a present that he had given them.

I think it's important to know that we are not perfect beings. I tell my class about the ethnic and racial slurs that I make about others. Here I am, a gay man making remarks about other minority groups. I hate it when people say, "Goddamn faggot." And yet I must stop myself from doing the same type of thing.

I admit to the students that I sometimes say to myself, "fucking nigger," or "fucking spik," or "fucking Jew," or "goddamn bitch." These are things I heard all the time in my home. They were knee-jerk reactions. The kids were shocked by my admission. I said, "Here I am asking you guys not to be prejudiced. And I find myself reacting the same way."

I reveal this for a reason. I say, "Even now I find these expletives coming out of me. I catch myself and say, 'I don't believe I thought that. I'm reacting to some inconsiderate jerk. A scumbag who just did something.' What should be coming out is 'scumbag,' rather than an ethnic slur. I have a lot of friends who are Jewish or black. I know that what I'm saying is not true. Yet it still comes out. It has become so ingrained in my past experience that it pops out automatically. But being an adult means that I must reason with myself. My reactions are wrong, unacceptable. I cannot say that." The kids hear me.

Gay kids need to have some kind of support group. They definitely need to know there is somebody they can talk to who won't judge them.

Rachel and I started a group in school. I tell the kids if they must fool around sexually, fool around with people your own age. And do it safely. Don't get into something you can't handle emotionally.

A professor of mine in graduate school encouraged us to think out loud in front of the kids. In that way they can see us grappling with ideas and issues. We need to teach students that they should not be afraid to not have an answer. For some issues there may not be an answer, there may just be a search.

The students here are very kind. One asked me if I was ever going to have my own kids. I told her, "I look at you guys as my kids." She smiled. Her eyes filled up. I really believe that. If you are a gay teacher and want to have kids, they are right in front of you.

CHAPTER **18**

Ethnic Heritage Day

O N the fifth floor, Ms. Williams tells her government class about some of Ethnic Heritage Day's events that will begin third period. "The African-American Club is conducting workshops on racism and stereotyping. Ms. King, who is the mediation counselor, is doing multicultural-conflict skits in the library. Humane Humanities will do a cultural trivial pursuit. There is a workshop that centers on the Jewish adolescent experience. There will be Chinese-character writing. And our very own students, Wai and Howard, will conduct a workshop about the Chinese immigrant experience called 'Coming to America.' "

Not to be left out, another student, Carey, says, "I'm doing a workshop on poetry from different cultures. I'm going to talk with students about how their poems differ."

"That sounds good," Williams replies.

Mr. Hirsch's English class is in full swing. The students had been instructed to ask a grandparent, or an older relative, to tell them something about their background that they never knew before.

A Bangladeshi, Peter Gomez, speaks first. He asked his family, "Since we are from Bangladesh, how come my father's last name is Gomez and my mother's name is Cruz?" His grandmother told him that about ten generations ago, Portuguese settlers migrated to Bangladesh. Peter's ancestors were among them. "When my parents visited Bangladesh, they went to our ancestors' grave. There were two Gomezes dating back to the eighteenth century."

"Does everybody know where Bangladesh is?" asks Mr. Hirsch. Many shake their heads "no." Zuzu calls out, "It's about seventy-five percent underwater."

Another teacher pokes her head into the room and asks if she can have Laura for a minute.

When Laura and a few volunteers from the other class return, they carry platters filled with various ethnic foods. "Breakfast, everybody," she sings out.

The assignment next door was for all the students to bring dishes that best represent their ethnic groups. The oversized platter is filled to the brim with noodle pudding, pasta, baklava, rice and beans, crepes, spare ribs, egg rolls, and more. Hirsch urges the students, "Don't eat the food from your own culture. Experiment." The students are particularly interested in the cinnamon-and-raisin noodle pudding, an Eastern European Jewish dish. After everyone fills his or her plate and returns to their seat, the conversation continues.

Hirsch, eating away, calls on people. "Mai Li?"

"Yes?"

"Talk to us."

Mai Li has always been quiet in the classroom. She speaks softly. "My mother told me that in China, on the first day of the month, you can't wash your hair. It is considered bad luck. I never knew that. She also told me that before the cultural revolution my grandfather was rich and owned land in Canton. Now it's gone."

Laura speaks next. "My paternal grandmother told me that to get out of Russia, she paid for an illegal passport by selling stockings and cigarettes on the black market. Although the black market was a dangerous thing to be part of, my grandmother had a big business going. She would go around Leningrad selling things. If she got caught, she would have been sent to Siberia. I never knew that she was a black marketeer."

Hirsch laughs as he bites into an egg roll. "Which means, Laura, that you come from a long line of criminals."

"That's right! It's in my blood." She laughs with the group.

"Anybody have anything to add about your own culture?

Gina raises her hand. "In Haiti, carnival is a big thing. During the month of February all the schools are closed. From morning till night you are on the street dancing."

Hirsch ties his students' anecdotes to instructional materials. "Isn't carnival part of the pre-Easter tradition of Lent?"

"It's like that in Peru," says a Peruvian-American student. "But in my country, carnival is every Sunday in February, not every day. Our carnival is not so good because the people throw things at everyone. They throw eggs. They throw water. They throw powder."

"Ugh!" groan the others.

When the bell rings, everyone hangs around for the last few mouthfuls of food. Now it is off to the workshops.

On the fifth floor, a session about stereotyping is being run by the African-American Club. Edwina, the leader of this session, says, "I find that there are preconceived ideas about how people look. For example, people say that Puerto Ricans can't be dark. Yet, I know lots of dark Puerto Ricans. Has anybody experienced that?"

The group is quiet, uncomfortable, and unwilling to speak out.

Another leader says, "In this school there is no racism, but outsi—" She is interrupted by snickers. She tries again. "Has anyone here experienced racism? Ever?" No one replies.

Edwina gets angry. "You've never experienced racism? In eighteen years? Come on now."

One boy finally says that he is sure everybody in the room has experienced some form of racism.

At last an Hispanic female dives in. "Remember when all those college representatives came to our school? I wanted information about Cornell. I went up to the white representative and asked her for some pamphlets and whatnots. She said, 'Well, you have to be real smart. You have to have a ninety average. And you have to have money, too, because it is a very expensive school.' I just wanted some information.

"I stepped back because I was so embarrassed. The next person to go up to her was white. When she asked for information, the woman said, 'We have this course, we have that course, etc.' She spoke very kindly to her. She didn't say you need money. She didn't say you need this and you need that. I felt bad. I guess she assumed that all Puerto Ricans are poor."

Another leader asks if anyone ever experienced racism from members of their family. A tall boy, in the middle of the room, says, "My father is

African-American and my mother is Puerto Rican. Since I have dark skin, people think I'm black. My mother has always made sure that I don't forget my Puerto Rican heritage. She makes sure that I think of myself as a Puerto Rican man as well as a black man. When it comes time for me to fill out an application form, I never know which 'race' box to check. I don't want to discredit my father or my mother. Sometimes I just write in 'both.' "

Now the group is warming up. A bashful African-American girl giggles nervously when she begins to speak. With muffled voice she says, "It was only after my parents were married, and I was already born, that my father learned that my mother's father was white. He became very angry. As a child he was taught not to associate with someone who is mixed. When he told my grandmother, his mother, that my mother's father was white, she became furious. Since that time I can't go and visit my father's family. They are really prejudiced against me. When they see me they throw things at me. One time, when my mother was away, they locked me out of my house."

As the student continues, her voice becomes stronger. "We all have the same blood in our veins. We all have the same organs. It's just a difference in hair color, accents, and skin color. That doesn't mean that we are so different." Everyone instantly agrees. Encouraged by the support from her classmates, she continues to speak. "Sometimes it is good to learn about these things at an early age. It prepares you for the future.

"When I go to Jamaica, or I travel somewhere else, almost everybody has the same tradition and culture. Here in New York City we're so diverse. Everybody's free to express themselves. Of course, there are some ignorant people who make racial remarks, but the majority of us are good." Everyone applauds when she sits down. And now everyone has something to contribute.

In yet another workshop, a Japanese girl is complaining because everyone assumes that she is Chinese.

Someone else confesses that she never tells people where she comes from because people think that all Colombians either sell drugs, sell coffee, or steal hubcaps.

"I feel discrimination every day," says Andrew, an Irish boy with carrot-red hair and freckles. This group appears determined to tackle racism head-on.

The teacher says, "I think all you guys have some real problems to face in your lifetime. Blacks are blaming whites for having money and whites are blaming blacks for committing crimes."

Mrs. Jarvis drops into the session and takes a seat with the kids. Rebecca, an outspoken white student, sits at the teacher's desk, and says, "I was taught that white people were better."

The teacher talks about his brother-in-law who lives in Connecticut. "The only thing he learns about New York is what he sees on TV. He thinks this place is an armed camp of drug dealers and race riots. He's a good friend of mine, but when I talk to him, he says things that are really racist. What can I say? He's my brother-in-law." The teacher shrugs his shoulders. "It is an uncomfortable situation."

Rebecca asks, "Do you think it is possible not to be prejudiced?"

Another replies, "I think it grows out of frustration."

"It's deeper than that," a student calls out. "When a fat person gets on a train, people stare and make fun of him. Where does frustration come into it? For some reason, people like being cruel."

Frank, a Puerto Rican senior, says, "People do tease each other about race, but then, you hear comedians like Eddie Murphy and Richard Pryor tease about race all the time. That makes us think that it's okay to do it, too. Blacks joke that all Hispanics are Rico Suave, a rapper, who I think is stupid.

"Eddie Murphy breaks on Spanish people and we think it's funny. Then, when kids do it in school, I don't take offense. If you really think about it, most Hispanics do do things like dance Marangue and stuff like that. Murphy jokes that all black people eat chicken. And then you go to Kentucky Fried Chicken and there are the black people, sitting there eating chicken. It's funny."

Everyone agrees that it helps when television takes on tough issues. The teacher says, "They are starting to portray gay people on TV shows, good shows like *L.A. Law*. A lot of people will see that gay people aren't freaks. Here in New York we see gays all the time, but someone from a place like South Dakota isn't used to it."

The teacher stops and thinks about what is being discussed. "The next time somebody in my family says something racist, I'm going to say how offensive those remarks are. They may not change, but at least I tried. And, all of us here, if we teach our kids not to be prejudiced, maybe we can turn things around."

In the afternoon there is dancing in the gym and a performance in the auditorium. An Indian dancer, dressed in a beautiful sari, performs a traditional dance in the center of the room.

"WOLF! WOLF! WOLF!" screams the happy crowd packed along the sidelines and in the bleachers.

A Latin American extravaganza is up next. Eight dancers, dressed in red, white, and black costumes, take their places around the gym. Music up. "The Lambada!" everyone screams.

The choreography is stunning. Most of the audience dance along in the bleachers. Like the kids, the teachers on the sideline wiggle and jiggle to the beat. The school guard cha-cha-chas in the corner. One of the female dancers pulls the dancing guard onto the dance floor with her. Other dancers grab their teachers. Everyone's a Michael Jackson in this school.

Afterward, when a reggae singer steps up to the mike, he invites the students to dance on the gym floor. As the music gets hot, the movements become sexier and sexier. Hips pulse. Chests heave. Bumping. Grinding. Dunking. Dipping. Heads dip below the waist.

Enter Ms. Williams! She serenely cuts in on one of the sexy dancers. Williams and her partner dance a bit more primly, but with great style. She calls to the kids around her to "have a good time, but cool it down a little." No one seems to mind her recommendation. A few even try to cool it. Everyone is having a wonderful time, except of course the girl whose boyfriend is now bumping and grinding in the arms of Ms. Williams. The girlfriend wants her man back. She stomps toward the sideline, but is snatched up by Mr. Schwartz, who whirls her around the dance floor.

Meanwhile, in the auditorium, Mrs. Jarvis announces the names of the Bayard Rustin essay contest winners. When the winner, an African-American, is called to read her essay, there is a huge round of applause. "Go, Kristen," the audience shouts. The second runner-up, Maya-Shanti, the Nepali student, is also asked to read her essay. She too gets a huge round of applause.

Finally Mrs. Jarvis gives a speech. Her eyes fill with tears. She tells her students how moved she was by their presentations. "I am so proud of all of you. Ethnic Heritage Day is our own special day. I hope it will go on forever and forever. I would like to read you one very, very short paragraph that means a great deal to me. It is a quote from Bayard Rustin. He says, 'The concept of human rights means that if I harm anyone, I am attacking myself at the same time. When I preach hatred against an Italian, or a Jew, or a Pole, I am also digging my own grave. That is because hatred makes it possible for people to do the same thing to me. My objective must be to eliminate hatred.' And that's what today is about. Today is about living up to those things which Bayard Rustin stood for. Thank you all. You are beautiful children.''

The bell rings and the students pour out of the auditorium. Another day at the Bayard Rustin High School for the Humanities has come to an end.

About This School

BAYARD Rustin High School for the Humanities is a college-preparatory school that serves District 2, a very large district in Manhattan. There is a staff of 130, ninety-three of whom are teachers. At the time this book was written, there were 1737 students. Ninety-two percent of the students go on to a four- or two-year college or to a professional school. The dropout rate is 4.3 percent.

Bayard Rustin lived in the community where the Charles Evans Hughes High School for the Humanities is located. In 1988 the parents and staff petitioned the Board of Education to rename the school in honor of Mr. Rustin. The principal, Mrs. Jarvis, says, "He was a person who really cared about humanity. He exemplifies for us some of the characteristics and the values that we try to instill in our youngsters: that we live in a global village, that as long as I am denied freedom, you are denied freedom, that we need to care about and reach out to one another. It is not enough to say I tolerate everybody, because 'tolerate' connotes a superior attitude." In 1989 the name of the school was officially changed to the Bayard Rustin High School for the Humanities.

About Bayard Rustin

BAYARD Rustin (1912–1987) was a political activist, socialist, pacifist, and an adviser to Martin Luther King, Jr. Among his many achievements was that in 1958 and '59 he coordinated the National Youth Marches for Integrated Schools, which pressed for full enforcement of the 1954 Supreme Court case of *Brown v. Board of Education*. Along with A. Philip Randolf, he conceived and organized the 1963 March on Washington for Jobs and Freedom, the massive demonstration where Dr. King made his "I have a dream" speech. A quarter of a million people from all over the country, of all races and religions, participated in what was then the largest demonstration for human rights in the history of the republic.